T0129847

OTHER TITLES BY ROY/RF/
ROY F. SULLIVAN

MURDER AT THE BEST LITTLE LIBRARY IN TEXAS

ROY SULLIVAN

authorHOUSE®

AuthorHouse™
1663 Liberty Drive
Bloomington, IN 47403
www.authorhouse.com
Phone: 1 (800) 839-8640

Published by AuthorHouse 01/09/2019

ISBN: 978-1-5462-7502-2 (sc)
ISBN: 978-1-5462-7512-1 (e)

Library of Congress Control Number: 2019900235

Print information available on the last page.

This book is a work of fiction, pure fiction. Any references to
real people, actual locales or businesses are used fictitiously.
Other names, places, lyrics, characters and incidents are
the product of the author's imagination. Any resemblance
to actuality is the result of chance, not intent.

Dedicated to Librarians Everywhere

ONE

I t was late September in the Hill Country of Texas, still hot and simmering, waiting for cooler temps or maybe a taste of rain to awaken the cedar-clad hills and dry pastures.

Monday morning and the streets of Carrville, Texas, were crowded with yellow Head Start school buses, behind them lines of impatient motorists waiting as bus doors opened to swallow sleepy school children struggling with backpacks.

Drumming slender fingers on the steering wheel, Lara lip-synched

> "*I got to get my rest,*
> *'Cause Monday's a mess!*"

Traffic creeped along narrow Water Street as she guided her late model sedan along with the pick-ups and SUVs. The stop light ahead on Main Street changed, allowing traffic to enter Highway 16, leading south to Bandera. At traffic intervals like this, she usually sang a happy alto. Fittingly, today's tune was 'Blue Monday.'

As soon as possible, Lara eased into the far right, causing a big black pickup following closely on her bumper to repeatedly honk in complaint. Loudly.

"I'm never sure" she said to herself, "if the honk is for me or for my car tag."

The tag proclaimed "**LIVE BETTER; READ MORE**"

Thinking positively, she waved a languid hand out the open window at the honker as she pulled into the parking lot of the library--*her* very own library for the last five years.

She backed the Ford into an empty space in the last row. "No assigned parking places for library employees," she reminded herself of the first new rule when she became Library Director.

She locked the driver's door and stood, checking her appearance in the window. Her coal black hair cut short was seldom a problem. Large luminescent green eyes--which could look either endearing or fiery--inspected her reflection, a slim image of a white, frilly blouse over black slacks and no-nonsense flats.

She'd prefer jeans, T-shirt and cowboy boots. 'Library Directors dress professionally,' she mouthed the phrase learned as a graduate student of library science at College Station where she attended A&M University.

As usual, her dependable chum and sounding-board, Amy Sidwell, chief reference librarian, already had opened the library side door and turned on the first floor lighting. Standing beside the coffee/break room, thirtyish Amy, blonde pony tail half-way down her back, smoothed a green skirt topped by an amber sweater.

"Morning," they smiled and spoke simultaneously as Lara dropped her black briefcase, another required accessory for library directors, on the coffee table.

"Coffee's makin'," Amy announced as she tasted the first cup. Making a face at the result, she asked, "How was your night?"

Lara deadpanned. "Dull and duller. The usual. Think I watched *Raymond* reruns until midnight."

Amy made another face. "Ouch!"

Lara flinched at Amy's look. "But you...you had a date with Harold last night. Right? How'd it go?"

Amy blinked blue eyes over the rim of her large cup. "Another tag match, but I won."

Lara rolled her eyes. "Thought you really liked the guy?"

Amy sniffed. "My calico cat's better company after the first few minutes. Harold's new passion is the NFL draft."

Sighing, she added a dollop of cream to her cup. "Talks about it nonstop."

Last week Amy mentioned a planned future cruise out of Galveston with Harold. "No more talk about that Caribbean love boat get-away?"

Amy sat, staring at the laptop. "Not until after the Super Bowl, he says. Then he'll come up with another excuse," she lamented.

Turning on a laptop, Amy shook her head. "What

about your latest adventures with Make-A-Match? Any handsome bachelor persistently vying for your in-box?"

Ignoring the innuendo, Lara picked up the day's schedule of library activities. "Doris handling the Children's Hour again?"

"Yep. she enjoys it, except for those bossy parents."

"Oh, for the life of a public librarian," Lara mimicked. "Work, work, work and not an eligible man in sight!"

Her voice raised an octave. "But the pay's good and going to get better after Christmas!"

"Yippee!" Amy jumped out of her chair. "You mean those commissioners approved your new budget? We'll get a raise?"

"That's the rumor, believe it or not. But don't order champagne until we have it in our hot little hands."

Slender, Doris Meeker, brunette bangs almost hiding her seriously-round reading classes, came through the door, momentarily posing for them in her new twist top and skinny jeans. She stopped, eyeing them suspiciously. "What's going on? You two look too friendly for Monday morning. What's wrong?"

"We're fine," Lara helped herself to *Mr. Coffee*. "Are you ready for the kiddies' hour? Need anything?"

Doris gestured. "Short a few blankets for the little darlin's sitting on the rug, but we'll be okay."

"I can get more," Lara volunteered.

"We'll be fine."

Clarice, the housekeeper, bustled in and paused,

overhearing the subject. "I'll keep an eye on the restrooms. They may need extra cleaning."

"Thanks, Clarice. Better keep a mop handy, too."

With a wave, Clarice disappeared into her supply closet, muttering "Roger that, Boss."

Lara refilled her cup as Susan and Eugenia, who manned the book check-out station, arrived and took adjoining chairs behind the check-out partition near the library front doors.

Doris did a mock salute as Lara waved at the newcomers. "All present and accounted for, Director. Except for our resident bachelor, Harry, who's on a week's leave ogling co-eds in Austin."

Lara half returned the salute with a grin. "Good report. For that you've earned the first two book salesmen this morning."

Doris elbowed Susan. "With my luck, the *sales men* will be *sales dollies*."

TWO

"Lara," slender Susan who'd just spent a week hospitalized for colitis, telephoned Lara's office from the front desk.

"There's a gentleman here wanting to see you. Shall I send him back?"

"Book salesman? Doris will handle him."

"No, he looks like a cowboy...or something. Named Roberts."

"Does the cowboy look dangerous? Wearing spurs?"

Susan took her time, looking over the tall man in faded levis standing there, grinning at her. She returned the smile with interest before pointing him down the hall toward Lara's open door.

"Grade A, I'd say," she giggled as the man turned away and started down the hall. "He's on the way. If you don't want him, send him back. *I'll take him,*" she whispered.

Lara rose to meet the stranger, pausing outside her door to read its "Library Director" inscription.

"How I help you, Mr. Roberts?"

He towered over her, white teeth glinting from a tanned face like a toothpaste commercial.

"You may not remember…. I'm the guy who honked at you yesterday morning as you pulled into the parking lot here. You waved at me.

"I thought to follow-up your friendly greeting. It took me a whole day to track you down."

She studied the man, unhappy with the memory of his loud honking from the pickup behind hers.

"As I recall you also gave me the famous finger greeting as you roared by in your big black dually. To add to that quaint insult, that big dog in your passenger seat howled at me!"

Roberts blinked at the onslaught. "I apologize for Pooch and me, Ma'm. I'm here, hoping to redeem myself over lunch with you. Even Library Directors," he grinned, again exposing perfect teeth, "require nutrition."

She stifled a smile. "No thank you, Mr. Roberts. Nice of you, but I don't intend to be fattened up and auctioned off at your sales barn."

In his best version of contrite, his smile faded. "I apologize for the honking and inappropriate display, Miss…?" He paused, looking at her sideways.

"Beyer," she provided her name. She stared at him. "Are you one of our library patrons, Mr. Roberts?"

He held up a just-issued library card. "Yes, Ma'm. So this proves I must be a reliable citizen. I repeat the offer. Please have lunch with me? I'm anxious to make amends as well as learn about what goes on in a big high-tech, attractive library like this." His eyes roamed the upper floors and computers above them.

"Thank you, Mr. Roberts, but we're having our staff luncheon today. I doubt you'd be interested in our library-oriented conversation and twitter that accompanies it. Have a nice day elsewhere. Goodbye now."

Later, at noon, she was so absorbed checking the September schedule of library activities, she didn't notice the amused silence of Amy, Doris, Susan and the others seated around the luncheon table.

In the center of the table, surrounded by the usual brown bags from home, cold drinks and snacks, sat a very large white layer cake decorated with little red flower buds and red lettering legible clear across the room.

Lara stopped and stared. "What's this?"

Some grinning, some giggling, the others all pointed at the bold lettering on the cake:

LARA: DINNER AT SEVEN PLEASE? DAN 257-5900

After only crumbs remained of the cake (everyone had seconds), Doris and Susan lagged behind in the lunch room, apparently to help Clarice clean up the luncheon mess. Their real purpose was to discuss the cake as an omen of their boss's future.

"That man is drop-dead devine!" Susan was the first to voice an opinion.

Clarice, vacuuming nearby, heard the whisper and seconded the motion. "He'd sweep her--me included-- off that library science pedestal!"

Doris volunteered. "If she doesn't go for him, I'm next in line." She swayed and began singing and gyrating:

> *"Take a chance on me!*
> *Take a chance on me!"*

Meanwhile Lara returned to her office, frowning at the telephone as she formed a mental reply to that presumptuous Mr. Dan Roberts. She already knew his first name after a quick scan of his library card application.

"Roberts here," he answered the first ring crisply. His voice and tone initiated alarm bells ringing somewhere within her starched, impregnable white blouse.

Highly unusual, she mentally conceded. Even frightening.

She recovered instantly and managed, "Mr. Roberts, this is Lara Beyer at the library."

He interrupted her prepared brief thank you with a "Dan, please."

"Mr. Roberts, I'm calling to thank you," she resumed, ignoring his offer, "for the lovely cake you sent our staff. It was a welcomed and thoughtful addition to our luncheon."

"My pleasure, Lara. I hope you like chocolate cake with white icing. I had to guess at that."

"It was perfect. Everyone," she emphasized the word, "really enjoyed your treat."

He paused, "You're welcome. But I'm hoping you called *not* to thank me for the cake but to accept my invitation for dinner this evening."

He pleaded again. "Please say yes, Lara. I especially need to talk to you about a project to assist the young people of my group to better use your library's facilities. They're young farmers and ranchers, unused to the modern complexities of a library. Your library."

An unexpected twist, she thought, reconsidering the polite 'no thanks' she'd prepared for this stranger. Lara played with a pen from the desk. "What kind of group?"

"It's the 4-H Club of Kandall County. We've enlisted over fifty youngsters in it."

She made a note. "What's your role, Mr. Roberts?"

"Dan, please," he repeated. "I'm just a sponsor. Be easier to explain," he paused, "over dinner.

How about it?"

She stalled. "Couldn't we handle the explanations at the library tomorrow? I can meet you at one after our Brown Bag Book Club event."

"'Fraid not." She could visualize a quick head shake as he said it. "Unfortunately, I have a long-standing appointment in Fort Worth in the morning."

"Well…" She wavered a second, thinking 'Alone with a man I don't even know?' She remembered the previous alarm bells.

"All right," she relented. "When and where shall we meet?"

"Yippee !" he exclaimed, reminding her of Amy's enthusiasm about the possible pay raise.

He followed up immediately, without giving her a chance to change her mind. "I'll be knocking on your front door at seven. Okay? You choose the restaurant since you know Carrville much better than me."

She almost corrected him. 'Than I,' she was thinking.

"Okay," was her cautious reply, hearing another tinkle of inward bells.

That evening, she opened the door at Roberts' knock and gasped.

"Oh, no," she mumbled, retreating into her apartment.

Dan Roberts was dressed in Sunday-dinner-after-church white shirt, tie, dark suit, and gleaming loafers.

Lara glanced down at her own Hill Country casual ensemble of skinny jeans topped by a boatneck sweater.

"I'll just go change," she began, starting up the stairs of her condo on West Broadway.

"Oh, no you don't!" He grabbed her and wrapped arms about her to prevent escape and change of her informal attire.

He tightened his hold on a surprisingly small waist. "You're not changing those comfortable, great looking clothes. We're dressed handsomely, especially you in that hot sweater!"

"I can't go like this…" she argued, "with you looking so…so formal."

He slammed the apartment door shut behind them and hustled her into his black pickup. Her initial fear was replaced by relief that the big barking dog was absent.

"Look," he still held her tightly to prevent escape (he told himself). "I thought we'd have steaks and you thought we'd have…?"

"Pizza," she dutifully completed his question.

"So we compromise like Washington politicians and go for Chinese instead of steaks or pizza. See? We're both dressed appropriately for…" he looked to her to fill in another blank.

"Roaring Dragon." She named a Chinese/Vietnamese restaurant in east Carrville.

By the time they were seated in a small corner table of the restaurant, the humor about their disparate attire subsided. They sat, studying each other across the small table as if seeing the other for the first time. As soon as their order was taken by the waitress, the laughter about their clothing revived.

Other diners stared at them inquiringly, sparking still more chuckles from the two.

"I'll long remember this date," he winked as tiny cups of tea were served.

Lara's smile disappeared. "This is *not* a date. This is merely a business arrangement for you to tell me how my staff can assist your 4-Hers."

Dan silently toyed with the small decorative table light without conceding. "Here come the egg rolls and 'Happy Family' entrée. Let's eat first, next get down to *business*, as you insist on calling it."

Concentrating on "business" wasn't that easy, he discovered. He wanted to know everything about this fascinating, attractive lady. Most women would be crowding him into a corner of the booth by now. He could barely repress his interest.

He began with an innocuous question about dessert, followed by a casual, "Born around here?"

"In Texas, but not here."

"Where?"

"Fort Sam Houston. I was an Army brat following my dad all over the world before he and Mom retired in San Antonio. And you?"

To his dismay, she had yet to call him Dan.

At least they were sharing information, he sighed. He was anxious to share much more than that. "I was born and raised in Comfort, just down the road."

Pleased with the opening, he inquired why she selected library science as a major.

Her eyes positively glowed, her voice animated, at the question. "I love being in a library. What a repository of all sorts of valuable information! Overused word, but *awesome* describes it!

"Now, add automation to the mix." She drew a deep breath. "An entire world of valuable data available to everyone, everywhere, via a few keystrokes!"

He shifted her enthusiasm to his group. "Our," he emphasized the word, "project will open that new and exciting world to these young men and women of the 4-H. You'll be their guide!"

Grabbing a napkin, Lara began writing and nodding.

"First, we'll familiarize them with the general layout and assets of the library. Then we teach them the capabilities of our twelve desktops available for their use. Maybe I'll need more. Each child should have easy access."

Dan touched then grasped a free hand. It seemed too easy. "We'll start them designing and running their own projects for 4-H credit."

Excitedly, Lara grabbed another napkin to continue her précis. "And divide them into small groups with a leader elected within each. They set their own pace! End up comparing and sharing their individual programs and projects!"

He held her hand tighter. "Could we invite health professionals in for occasional conferences? Maybe get a mayor or someone in to talk about citizenship?"

"Absolutely! And get them out in our library playground to end each meeting with fresh air and exercise!"

Later he expertly lifted door keys from her grasp and unlocked her apartment door, hoping for an invitation inside. This time he wasn't thinking about asking more questions.

Lara hid a yawn, inserting herself between him and the threshold. "Tomorrow's an early one for me," she murmured. "Art and science registration starts at eight and that's my chore as director.

"Thanks for a nice evening. I think we've a good start on your 4-H project."

He leaned forward to buss her cheek but she was already inside. He was barely able to ask 'See you day-after-tomorrow?' before the door slammed.

Rolling his eyes, he sighed and turned to go.

Just then the door reopened and Lara appeared with a shy smile. "Maybe you can come by the library that day at ten? That's just before I convene the leggo club at eleven. We can review what we've decided so far about your project."

THREE

"Got no time for talkin'
Got to keep on walkin'
'Cause I'm walkin' to New Orleans"

Lara sang the only lyrics she remembered to the tune that had been on her mind since awakening. She glanced at the rear mirror before guiding her car into the library parking lot and a vacant space on the back row.

"Nope," she acknowledged after checking the rear mirror. "No big black pickup following me. Wonder if Dan Robert's back from Fort Worth by now?"

This morning Doris, wearing plaid leggings, met Lara at their staff coffee bar. "You look different today, Boss. Did you accept that gorgeous man's dinner invitation last night?"

Lara gratefully accepted a cup of coffee from faithful Doris, not only one of her best friends but a mentor as well.

"Yeah, I did, but it was strictly business about his 4-H project."

Doris pursed her lips. "No time for …?"

"No, Doris. All business. Thanks for the coffee."

Cup in hand, Lara paused. "I bet our gifted, literary librarian knows what word describes the tune you wake up with and that you keep mentally repeating all day long?"

Doris grimaced with the effort, thumping her forehead gently. After several thumps, she smiled broadly.

"Too easy, Library Director! Everyone beyond the sixth grade knows the appropriate word is 'earworm.'"

Lara applauded. "Thanks, Doris! You are a genius!"

At that, Doris turned business. "Remember, we have the Art and Science registration at eight. You plan on being there to marshal that crowd?"

"Sure. If that Mr. Roberts shows up this afternoon to discuss his project, please give him a cup of coffee and park him anywhere you like."

"Boss," Doris winked, "you know exactly where I'd like to park that man."

"Okay by me if you want to live dangerously. Just don't let the staff see the two of you singeing the library stacks."

After the library opening at nine, Doris paused at Susan's station. "Guess what?"

Susan looked over the rim of her huge glasses. "I'm not good at puzzles this early. What's up?"

"Be wary around the boss lady today. I think she may be smitten and not even realize it."

"You mean by that tall, skinny cowboy?"

"That's the one, but he doesn't look skinny to me. To test my supposition, I volunteer to take it for a test drive."

As they talked, an elderly balding man wearing an old-fashioned monocle, stopped beside them. "Can one of you young ladies tell me how to occasionally rent your largest conference room?"

Doris nodded first. "It's available on a first-come-first-served schedule. There's no fee for library activities, like book study groups, using it."

"My name," he inclined his head at Doris, "is Donitz and I represent the local chapter of the Frederick 1 Society. The Society is composed of descendents of the German King, Frederick 1. We study his governance of what was glorious medieval Germany."

Doris studied the short man dressed in dark suit, vest and tightly-knotted green tie. "Is your chapter large?"

Donitz twittered, "Not at all. We have only five members locally but members from other cities and states join us from time to time. Our meetings are quite small since membership is not open to the general public. Rest assured, we would not disturb or distress your other library patrons."

"Have you a written description of your society for our Library Director?"

His smile exposed gilded dentures. "Indeed, I do." He offered a small pamphlet with his calling card.

"Thank you, Mr. Donitz. I'm sure our Director will contact you shortly to discuss your request."

Donitz clicked his heels, causing everyone on the first floor to start at the noise and look around. The movement was so sudden that his monocle almost popped out.

"Good day, ladies," he inclined his head again and departed.

Susan and Doris looked at each other, trying not to grin at the strange man and his monocle. Instead, they high-fived. "Wait 'til we tell Lara about this guy. She'll be sorry to have missed him because of that Arts and Science registration."

Amy Sidwell, sitting at the reference desk, looked up as a familiar figure came through the front doors. It was the one of the elderly men who daily troop to the library to read the latest financial papers. The *Wall Street Journal* was their most coveted prize.

The individual who claimed it first in the morning usually studied its pages for hours before relinquishing it to the next-in-line reader. The waiting reader (s) sat there, cracking knuckles, rustling less important financial/business publications, and frowning at the person possessing the *Journal.*

Their unspoken but clearly understood dictum to that lucky reader was "Hurry up!"

The first *Journal* reader this morning happily took a chair after urging Amy at the reference desk to have a good morning.

It was bearded Charley Moss, wearing faded blue overalls and red bandana. He carried a small jug of water to prevent having to use the water fountain in the library's corner. This assured him of continuous ownership of the *Journal* until he read it completely and was willing to pass it on to the next gray-hair or balding colleague.

Amy straightened up. "What happened to you, Charley?"

She motioned to his elbow covered by a thick plaster cast. It made the elbow stick out at an odd angle from his overalls.

"Oh, nothing," Charley blushed, trying to hide the elbow and cast behind him.

"Looks serious," she persisted.

One of Charley's companions behind him guffawed. "Yesterday, he raised his drinking arm one too many times. Now he's handicapped with a cast, making him a temporary teetotaler."

Charley spluttered and blushed. Clumsily, he shook the folded *Journal* apart and slid into his usual chair, ignoring the detractor.

Doris referred to the elderly reading group as the 'Wall Street Snorers.' Amy chose a different name for the half-dozen old men who sat around the table next to the reference librarian's desk, reading the financial publications. Some of them invariably fell asleep at the table until awakened at noon. Amy's name for them was the 'Financial News Nodders.' The unelected spokesman of the group, usually the first to grab the day's *Journal,* was Charley. Taking his duties seriously, he spoke in an official tone to the others.

"Dow's down 55 already."

Another of the 'nodders' added, "NAS is up 27 and likely to go higher by noon."

A voice angrily disagreed. "You can't know that for a certainty, Henry. Read what the *Market Monitor* said today."

An hour later, several of the nodders were dozing peacefully, if precariously, in their chairs when awakened by a loud cry.

"HELP, HELP! I CAN'T GET OUT!"

FOUR

Susan and Eugenia at the check-out desk were the first to respond.

"Did you hear that?" Fearfully, they looked at each other.

"Where did it come from? Who's yelling?"

Clarice, the housekeeper, tilted her head to better hear another, even louder, anguished cry.

"HELP ME! I'M CAUGHT AND CAN'T GET OUT!"

Clarice pointed toward the first floor restrooms. "There! That's where!"

Seizing the initiative, she motioned to Eugenia. "Hey, come with me! Someone's in trouble in one of the restrooms."

By now, the entire library staff was on its feet, responding to Clarice's command.

They halted in front of the restrooms, male to the left, female to the right.

"Which one?"

"WHERE ARE YOU?" Clarice bellowed.

The responding cry, clearly male, came from the men's room.

"Not me!" Eugenia held up both hands. "I'm not going in there!"

"It's not Afghanistan," Susan chided. "it's just a male restroom. Buck-up! Carry-on!"

Everyone quickly scanned the crowd standing before the two doors. No males in sight.

"Someone's got to go in there, quick!"

Doris pointed at Clarice. "You go! You go in there all the time for cleaning!"

"Not me!" Clarice balled a fist. "Might be some naked, crazed male in there, just waiting for a good-looker like me!"

"He may be seriously injured," Amy offered.

"In a bathroom?"

"Sounds like…maybe hemorrhoids," an 'I've been there' comment was whispered.

"Somebody should go in there right away!" Susan searched the other female faces without result.

"Get Lara! Where is she?"

"Third floor conference room," frowning, Doris answered. "Probably didn't hear a thing up there. Guess it's up to me."

She pointed at Amy. "You, you come in there with me! And bring your cell phone. We may need to call 911."

Holding their breaths, they burst inside the men's room.

It was empty, except for Charley Moss hunched over a commode, eyes imploring for help.

He spoke indistinctly for some reason. "Gee me out of dis thang."

Doris and Amy stopped feet away, staring as if he were a wounded animal.

Doris broke the trance. "What are you doing in that toilet, Charley? You sick?"

Breathing heavily, Charley answered in the same strange voice. "No, dammit! Dopped ma teet in dere."

Once they understood his problem, they couldn't resist laughing in unison, "You dropped your false teeth in the toilet?"

"Try kissing us, Charley Moss, and you're road kill," Amy tittered.

Doris was more pragmatic. "What's your arm doing in that toilet?"

Red-rimmed eyes glaring, Charley fumed. "Dis ain't funnee! My elbo caasts caught in here an I can't get it out."

Holding each other up to prevent falling, Amy and Doris stood there, gasping for breath.

Doris was the first to recover and inject a little order.

"Amy, call 911. Tell them we need the emergency rescue team from the Fire Department to come right away, to... extract... this patron who's caught in a toilet. I'll stay here with him until they arrive. Keep the others out."

Amy nodded and turned toward the door. "Also I'll send someone to tell Lara on the third floor so she'll know what's happening before the fire guys arrive. Their big noisy red truck will turn this place into a circus, with TV and all the trimmings."

"Go back to your places," Doris heard Amy tell the others outside the restroom door. "Clear the way! Help is coming. Back to your seats, please. And quiet! *This is a library!*"

"Just another day at the boring public library," Amy said to herself, checking her watch, wishing it were quitting time.

Seeing a frantic Lara surrounded by TV cameramen and reporters outside the library, Dan hustled and pushed through them, trying to shield her from the noisiest and most persistent. Police lined Water Street, directing traffic through the roadblock caused by a fire truck, an ambulance now entering the parking lot and a large TV van with ears.

As he pulled her inside the front door, there an onslaught of yelled questions and smart phones aimed at them. Dan succeeded in holding the big door shut behind them.

A large man wearing a longhorn-embossed T-shirt beat on the closed door yelling "You can't keep us out! This is a public library!"

"What's going on?" Dan asked a pale and shaken Lara.

Seeing her look, he added, "Tell me later."

As suddenly as they had appeared at the front door, the reporters and cameramen ran toward the side parking lot. One of them spotted a loaded stretcher being hustled out the side door and toward the ambulance.

One of the ambulance EMTs was shaking his head, ignoring a noisy barrage of questions.

"Who is he?

"What happened to him?"

"Are there more injured inside?"

"Was there a bomb in the library?"

"Was this a terrorist attack?"

Ignoring the questions, the EMTs slid the heavy stretcher into the back of the ambulance, slammed the door shut and left the parking lot, siren wailing.

Doris met Lara and Dan at the front door. "It's near closing time, Boss. Let's send everyone home and go soak our feet."

Lara recovered enough to hug Doris. "Great job! Thank you for taking charge. Is Charley going to be okay?"

"The firemen had to saw-off part of his cast to get him out of the john, but he's all right. They took him to the hospital to get a new cast."

"*With* his false teeth?

Doris chuckled. "Yes, with those stinky false teeth in his pocket. They're not yet back home in his mouth,

I hope. Charley has plenty to say with or without teeth. Wait 'til he shows up tomorrow to read the *Journal*!"

That evening Lara and Dan sat at an outdoor table at the Margaritas restaurant.

"Chivalrous for you to rescue me, even whisk poor little me away to dinner," her look combined caution and appreciation. "You seem to have been my knight in shining armor. Thank you. Obviously, I'm owing. How was your trip to Fort Worth?"

He passed her an oversized menu. "Compared to what's been going on at our local library today, Fort Worth was uneventful and boring."

He leaned closer over the narrow table. "Feeling any better? How about a margarita?"

She shook her head to the drink. But she answered his first question.

"No, I'm not. I'm just now realizing how the newspapers and TV will portray our library tomorrow. How will those crusty old commissioners--who've never been inside the library, by the way--react? Libraries aren't supposed to be scenes of chaos, fire and rescue."

She leaned back in the cushions and, reflectively sipped an iced tea.

"I doubt you realize, Mr. Roberts..."

"Dan," he interrupted for the tenth time.

"Okay, Dan, that our little library is a cauldron of unexciting but wonderful efforts. We teach children how to appreciate art and music. How to play--not confront--one another. We give the mothers a break from their daily routines and the chance to share experiences. We sponsor all types of daytime activities for the elderly, the lost and the befuddled."

She leaned forward, daring him to blink.

"Smile if you like, Mr. Roberts, but we are an all-purpose library, the best one around thanks to the efforts of our small, dedicated, perfectly marvelous staff.

"And now an incident like this happens! Makes us look like buffoons. An elderly library patron stuck in a toilet! Fire/rescue and police rush to the aid of the hapless female librarians!

"Maybe I'll have a margarita after all," she sat back in the chair, still measuring him.

"Wow!" he exclaimed. "You made your case! I didn't realize how much a library contributes to its community. I really admire and respect that..."

He wanted to add 'and especially you.'

Instead he ordered margaritas.

FIVE

Playfully, Doris challenged Lara the next morning. "You were seen cavorting last night at a local restaurant with Dan the Man. Anything titillating to share with your ole buddy?"

"Strictly platonic, buddy, and you're *not* old! I think I scared him off permanently with my monologue about how gifted we librarians are."

"Seen the morning paper yet?" Doris offered her a copy.

She pointed to the headline in the *Reporter:*

LIBRARY PATRON RESCUED

The article following the top of page headline began,

"At 3:40 yesterday the Fire Department Emergency Team responded to a telephone appeal from the Library to free a patron from a male restroom.

The patron, later identified by Peterson Hospital as Charley Moss of 2314 Maple Avenue, Carrville, was treated and released hours later. Confidentiality prevents the hospital from disclosing the specific treatment received without the patient's consent. Mr. Moss, a well-known and long term Carrville resident, declined consent as well as an interview with this reporter.

A library spokesperson stated "A patron had a minor incident in a lavatory. The Fire Department was notified and is commended for its quick response," she said. "Thanks also for the reaction of the Police Department which provided traffic control along Water Street adjoining the Library."

A black and white photograph accompanying the article showed several personnel surrounding the library's front door, demanding information. Another photograph illustrated the Emergency Medical Team headed by Lieutenant Malcolm Frazier in action. The EMT carried a man on a stretcher to a waiting hospital ambulance.

It was a "minor affair" claimed Frazier who expressed "pride in the timely and expert professionalism exhibited by every member of my team."

"Whew," Lara breathed. "How do you think the commissioners will take this…incident, as you wisely labeled it? Thanks, Doris! You represented our Library very well."

Doris sipped a coffee before pursing her lips as if it were too hot. "They'll demand a detailed report, maybe even question you at their next meeting. I'll bet the whole thing will be forgotten in a few days.

"With that out of the way, I should brief you on a few minor items."

Wearing a relieved look, Lara nodded as Doris checked her notes.

"First, Eugenia called in sick today. She was upset, she said, by the bathroom fracas yesterday and asked for 24 hours of annual leave to recoup."

"Okay. Susan can handle check-out all by herself?"

Doris nodded. "If she gets bogged down, Amy and I will pitch-in. But we don't expect unusual traffic today despite yesterday's toilet terror.

"Next on my list, Clarice says we have a leaking water pipe in the kitchen which she'll fix today or call the plumber if she can't do it herself. By the way, Clarice was an absolute brick yesterday. She has our now-famous men's restroom all cleaned up, of course."

A sudden, unexpected grin gave Doris away.

Recognizing the look, Lara leaned forward. "What?"

Straight-faced, Doris replied. "Clarice asked if we shouldn't have a small ceremony to dedicate that particular toilet with a small plaque containing Charley's name and yesterday's date. Maybe make it a staff party, suitably fitting that auspicious event?"

Lara clapped her hands. "You're funning, right?"

"No, Ma'm," Doris turned momentarily serious. "Your hard-working, seldom complaining staff works an average of 54 hours a week and seven days a week.

"How many hours over 54, *you* personally put in, I don't know," Doris added. "But it's a lot!"

Lara sat back in the director's chair, nodding. "You're saying this crazy ceremony would be a fun way to put the terror toilet in its proper perspective? That we all need a good laugh?"

Lara bit an index finger. "Not a bad idea, BB. It's plain you've put a lot of thought into this already. Who's going to plan the details of this gala event?"

"Amy would be good. She's got a great sense of humor. Remember when she told the joke about the strongest muscle in the male body?"

Lara's chuckle erupted into laughter.

"Great! Let's do it!"

> *"I'm ready, I'm willin'*
> *I'm able,*
> *To rock and roll all night..."*

She turned the volume down as she coasted to a stop on Guadalupe Street beside a familiar figure the next day.

"Very familiar," she sighed.

"Get in, Charley. Where ya' going?"

Charley Moss peered in the side window. Seeing it was Lara, he stepped back. "You may not want to give me a ride--especially to your library--seein' the trouble I caused there yesterday."

"Get in, Charley," she leaned over to push open the door. "I'm always happy to see you."

After he settled in the passenger seat, he stared ahead, hesitant to look at her.

Finally, he stammered. "I'm real sorry for what happened. I sure didn't mean to be a problem for you and the Library. I'm real anxious to...to redeem myself."

She glanced at him and grinned. "We know you're a good man, Charley. We value your patronage at the Library. As soon as we get there, I'm going to ask a favor of you. Two favors, actually."

"Yes, Ma'm. I'm here to help the Library in any way."

She led him down the hall to her office and motioned for him to take a chair.

Charley sat down gingerly, looking about him and removing his Spurs baseball cap. He'd never been in the director's office before.

Lara took out a pad and pen. "First, Charley, I want you to tell me how your teeth ended up in the john yesterday. I need this for my report to the commissioner's about our little accident."

"I can't! It's too embarrassing, Ma'm."

"I know, Charley. Maybe it'll be easier for you to write it down?"

"Don't think so. Sorry, but I can't put down words right. Sometimes I can't even read my own writing."

"Maybe you can tell me what happened in there by closing your eyes as if I weren't here? Try that, please.

"Shut your eyes and just tell me how your teeth fell into the toilet."

Eyes shut so tightly that his face cringed as in pain, he asked. "Think I can manage that. Is that all you need?"

"Yep, it's a good start."

"Well, I was standing there in front of the john, suddenly hiccupped and *out* they came and fell into the toilet."

"Anything else?"

"You know I tried to grab 'em before they splashed into the toilet, but my elbow got caught in the bowl because of that plaster cast on it. Then, the firemen came and got me out. That's it."

Lara rubbed her forehead, taking notes. "That's all?"

"May I open my eyes now?"

"Yes, Charley. Open your eyes. You did very well. Thank you."

She studied his pinched face. "Like to read, Charley?"

"I read the *Journal* every day!"

She drew a long breath. "Do you have grandchildren, Charley?"

"Yes, Ma'm, but they ain't in Carrville."

"Ever read stories to them?"

He relaxed slightly while patting the hole in his overall-covered knee. "Yep, I do. They like it, too."

"I have an idea, Charley, of how you might redeem yourself, as you put it, to the Library for your gambol yesterday. I need a mature man like you to read stories to our 4-6 year old children here at the library. You say you like reading to your grandchildren occasionally. Would you consider reading to a small group of kids here?"

She quickly added. "It would be on a trial basis, of course. Amy would be with you to help and see how the children respond to you."

'With a grandfather figure like you, they ought to be delighted,' she was thinking.

"You would have to be very neat and clean, Charley, since children are so impressionable. No smoking or chewing, either."

Charley Moss sat taller. With each new qualification, he nodded. "Sure, I could do that. When would I start my...test?"

"We offer 'Storytime' as we call it every Wednesday from ten in the morning until eleven. I'll see if Amy's available now to explain everything and show you samples of the readings.

"Sound all right?"

"Sure, if..." Charley hesitated.

"What?"

"I still get first crack at the *Journal*, don't I?"

Leaving Amy and Charley talking about 'Storytime' Lara hurried to the front where the Leggo Club was meeting in the reference area. Looking embarrassed, Doris rose from her desk.

"Something I forgot to mention to you, Boss.

The toilet caper still has me numb. That's my excuse, anyway."

"A gentleman," she nodded at an older, dapper man seated at a computer terminal, "asked if he could reserve the Conference Room for his club."

"That place is getting to be more popular, isn't it?" Lara encouraged Doris with a pat on the shoulder. "What did you tell him?"

"I said you'd call him with your decision. Now he's shown up before I could brief you."

"Is there a problem? What's his club?"

"Something about a study group on medieval Germany and its king. The funny thing is, he says his club meetings are not open to the public."

Lara nodded at the glass-enclosed Young Adult reading room. "Let's nip in here and talk. I have a couple more items for you, too."

Doris' eyebrows spoke the question. "Why here?"

"Gotta' tell you!" Lara began. "Charley's back! He and Amy are discussing his reading our Storytime sessions on Wednesdays. If he can do it okay--and he seems enthused--we'll continue him. Amy's now grilling him on Storytime in my office. If he performs well next Wednesday, we'll have slightly less workload for our already slim staff. What do you think?"

Doris's lips pursed. "Sounds too good, Lara. But how are we going to pay him?"

"Well," Lara bit her lip, suddenly thinking abut Dan Roberts. She had to ask, "What did you say?"

"How do we pay Charley? How do we fund it?"

Lara dismissed the thought with a wave. "He says he owes us for his lavatory incident. If he does Storytime well, we'll later pay him by miscellaneous voucher for each session. He may lose interest and quit after a few weeks."

"Can we talk about that guy at the terminal who keeps glancing our way?"

"Sure. That's the one who wants to use the Conference Room for some history group? You have doubts?"

"I do, Boss. He says his name is Donitz and he's some kind of an officer in this group studying..."

Doris made parenthesis marks in the air with her fingers. "Medieval Germany during the reign of some old king named Frederick.

"He left us a pamphlet on the group which is on your desk."

"What's the problem?"

"He even offered to pay us for the room, although he says he only has a half-dozen or so members and they meet only occasionally."

Doris turned her head away. "Besides that, just look at him sitting out there, monocle and all. He's straight out of the *Munsters*. You want a half-dozen like him wandering around the library, frightening pets and small children?"

Nodding, Lara chewed on a nail. "We'll give him one of our application forms to complete, then make a decision and keep it for fall-back if the commissioners ever challenge or question us.

"Speaking of the commissioners," Lara offered a paper. "Here's my draft report to the commissioners about our toilet turmoil. Talented you... knowing what 'earworm' means... easily can improve my hasty draft. Please mark it up and return it. We'll send it over to the city hall, hopefully never to hear of the famous toilet trick again."

Doris began reading the draft as Lara rose to leave.

"Wait!" she giggled. "Is this the honest-to-God-truth?"

"Charley's own words," Lara paused. "What's funny?"

"He says he lifted the lid, did his business, flushed, then sneezed his teeth down the crapper and dived in after them?"

Doris' laughter was contagious. Lara joined her, laughing so hard, visualizing Charley in action, that she had to sit again.

Charley was leaving her office as Lara entered. "Great smile, Charley! Are those your new teeth?"

Blushing, he scampered from the room without replying.

Lara sat in the visitor chair, nodding at Amy seated behind the desk. "How'd it go with our Storytime prospect?"

Amy tapped a pencil on her teeth before replying. "He may be a winner. He's certainly psyched-up to be our new reader. We'll see how he does on Wednesday.

I loaned him several story books. The two of us even did a short practice session."

She held up a yellow post-it, winking knowingly. "You got a call from that skinny cowboy--what's his name?"

Lara caught her breath. She'd been hoping for a call from Dan. "Guess you mean Mr. Roberts, about 4-H business," she emphasized the last word.

SIX

One hour later Dan Roberts and another man stood in front of her desk.

Roberts began. "Miss Beyer, this is John Schoolfield, chairman of the Carr County 4-H Club and an old Army buddy. I told John about the tentative plans we talked about for my Kandall County 4-Hers. John also is interested in the library project you and I outlined. He hopes his young 4-Hers can be included, too."

Lara gestured toward the chairs at her small conference table and they sat down. "How many youngsters are in your program, Mr. Schoolfield?"

Schoolfield cleared his throat and set a broad-brimmed hat on the table. "I have 32 kids at the moment."

She pulled stapled packages from her desk. "I word-processed these notes from our earlier discussion," she regarded Dan, neglecting to mention the discussion had been during a cozy dinner. "Hopefully, I included all the topics appropriate to a 4-H program here at the Library."

She frowned. "I did it late one night, so please overlook the typos."

Schoolfield reached for a copy. "You have a fine library here, Miss Beyer."

"Thank you."

They spend the next minute reading her notes

Dan was the first to look up. "I like it."

Schoolfield hesitated. "I like it, too, but remember," he looked at Dan, "the national program is centered about 'STEM,' meaning science, technology, engineering and math."

Dan bit his lip. "This is a first draft, John, not supposed to be all-inclusive.

With Miss Beyer's approval, we later add more topics."

"We may have a space problem with both your contingents," Lara injected. "Kandall County's 50 youths plus Carr County's 32 may have to be divided. The capacity of our largest room here is 50, max."

Schoolfield raised a finger. "Since the library is in Carr County, I hope my kids would get equal treatment."

Dan grimaced but managed a smile for Lara. "John and I can work this out. I suggest that we," he looked at Schoolfield, "get together this afternoon and draft a new listing of topics plus how to solve the space problem."

Seeing Lara frown, he arose. "Thanks for bringing that up."

Schoolfield nodded and the two men left the office.

Lara felt like leaning back and putting her gaucho pants and cowboy boots on the table. "Maybe hot coffee will revive my cautious optimism. We seem to have more entanglements in this quiet little library than in a Galveston fishing tournament."

Several weeks before, a small gathering of men met in a hotel in Fort Worth, Texas. After a dozen silent men filed into the room and took seats in front of a podium, the man standing at the front spoke.

"Close the door, Bruno. You already ran the detection gear? Are we clear here?"

"We are, sir." With that Bruno took his customary hands-in-pockets stance, guarding the room's only entrance.

"Then I call this meeting to order," Donitz surveyed the dozen faces, flushed from the beer, brats and *brotchen* private luncheon preceding their meeting in one of Fort Worth's finest hotels.

"One of you questioned why we are openly...or so to speak...meeting in this well known hotel," he glanced around at their faces, one of which flinched at his gaze.

"My answer is that we are best hidden by being in apparent public view," he stared at them. "I appreciate your timely arrival today despite the short notice. As reported, this is a mandatory meeting of our order to consider a new method of achieving our historic mission: discovering and punishing the descendants of those responsible for the defeat and defamation of our noble sovereign.

"You may not make notes of this meeting, photographs or any type of digital recording of our deliberations. By a show of hands, you may now signal your understanding and unequivocal agreement with this rule."

A silence fell as hands were dutifully raised around the polished oval table. The leader studied each face as hands were raised.

"Thank you, hands down," he spoke after acknowledging their unanimous consent.

"All of you are aware, through the annals of TV and the on-line computer, of the success of private companies offering genealogical research to an eager public. For a relatively small fee, these private companies offer to trace an individual's DNA ancestry back many generations.

"We intend to use genealogical testing as a method of locating the descendants, if any, of the Lombard League in northern Italy responsible for their treacherous defeat of our blessed King and Kaiser, Frederick 1."

He ignored several raised hands around the table.

"Once identified, we will decide the fate of those descendents. It is our holy and sworn duty to do so, the very purpose since establishment of our order.

"Now, I'll attempt to answer a few questions."

After a pause a hand raised.

"Yes?"

"Our revered King Frederick 1 was born in the 1100's..."

"Eleven hundred and twenty-two, to be exact," Donitz interrupted.

The questioner nodded at the correction. "How, sir, is it possible for a modern civilian corporation to take a swab of spittle and determine the genealogy of an individual back to the time of our revered King Frederick? It sounds like extreme, imaginary science-fiction."

Nodding at his table companions for support, the questioner sat down with an concerned expression.

Donitz smiled. "An excellent question. Here's my simple lay explanation. The DNA in your mouth can be scientifically analyzed by means I can neither comprehend nor explain.

"The Y chromosome is found in DNA of the male of our species. Study of that Y chromosome may reveal a haplogram. The haplogram points out the geographical area of the world where that DNA is found in high frequency. The haplogroup area we are concerned with is the northern Italian city of Pavia, capital of the nefarious Lombards."

Although he nodded to encourage more questions, the audience seemed stunned by an overload of information. Eventually, another hand was raised at the end of the table.

"Yes?"

"How do we obtain information on an individual from the genealogical firm? It would seem to me that the firm has a legal and ethical obligation to safeguard any information developed from the customer's individual DNA."

Donitz nodded approvingly "Another excellent question. We are fortunate to have a member of our order employed in a high position within one such, nameless firm.

"He, or she, provides us the data on any individual sharing the particular Y-chromosome carried by Lombard males.

"We investigate the identified individual, who might possibly reside in our own state, city, even neighborhood. Once satisfied about the accuracy of our information, we simply and quietly *eliminate* that individual."

Prepared for the collective gasp of alarm of the audience, he eyed their slack faces. "Have you forgotten the oath taken when you joined our order? To seek revenge on those who defeated and derided our king?"

Donitz grabbed his wine glass and held it aloft.

"To our King and Emperor, Frederick 1!"

SEVEN

Susan and Eugenia sat in the coffee room, enjoying their half cups to the last. "Sometimes I just hate sitting there," she nodded at their checkout station, "waiting to check out a book they could have done all by themselves at the terminal."

Susan nudged Eugenia. "Don't you?"

Eugenia swallowed the last of her coffee and tossed the plastic cup in the trash. "Sure. If they all used the check-out machine, I'd have plenty of time to critique what they're wearing.

"Can you imagine? Yesterday I saw an orange sports bra under a purple lace top! And she was wearing Nike goldtops, too!

"Look here," Eugenia passed her phone to Susan to show her the photo she'd secretly made of yesterday's high fashion winner.

"Wow," Susan responded, withdrawing her own phone from a jean hip pocket. "Your fault, showing me that photo! Now I'v got to show you one of my adorable little Betsy, age five."

Eugenia held Betsy's photo closer. "She's adorable!

And so big! Last time I saw her at the library picnic, she was a toddler."

Susan yelped. "Let me tell you the joke that toddler told me after school yesterday.

"What kind of bear has no teeth?"

Eugenia shook her head. "Don't know."

Susan doubled over laughing before she exploded with her daughter's punch line. "A *gummi* bear!"

Interrupting their laughter, Amy opened the coffee room door and motioned. "Come and give me a hand, please. We've got a sudden run on returned overdue books!"

Their foul dispositions and angry looks dampened conversation as they rode the elevator to the second floor of the City Hall. The council usually met the second and fourth Tuesday of each month. But at 6:00 p.m., not on an afternoon!

What in the world are we doing here, each mentally groused. Gathering for a special meeting on Saturday afternoon! A football Saturday afternoon!

Rob Spokes, the senior commissioner, acting as chair, motioned. "Sit down, sit down and let's get this business over with as soon as possible."

"What is so pressing that we had to meet today?" Ed Wench, just elected to council seat four, was brave enough to voice what older hands dared not.

"It's that toilet business over at the Library, Ed. Anyone here *not* heard about that fracas?"

The nods were dour but unanimous. No one would

admit not hearing (and rehearing) about the Library toilet "incident' as the *Daily Reporter* phrased it.

Spokes looked placated by their expressions. "Alright, then, let's get to it and out of here in record time. In front of you are the reports of the toilet mishap from the three agencies involved: the Police, the Fire Department and the Library.

"Since I'm the only one with the chance to read these reports, I'm going to give you a brief 'Spokes summary.' Is that agreeable? Or shall we take the time for everyone here to read these three lengthy reports?"

"Very well," Spokes said looking around the table. "The first one, and easiest, is the police report."

At that moment, the door to the council's sanctum opened and several elderly men wearing baseball caps and work clothing silently trooped in and took seats along the margins of the room.

Spokes, took off his glasses to study them. "Gentlemen," he began, "this is a private, called meeting of your council, discussing important city business. Please leave at once!"

One of the gray-haired men stood up, noisily clearing his throat. "We're all tax-paying city residents," the wave included his fellows. "We have a right to be here to see what you're up to."

Another man also stood. "We're library patrons and you'd better not be fooling with our library." There was scattered applause from the other elderly men.

With that the second man sat down, leaving the first in place.

Spokes chuckled, looking to his colleagues for support against these intruders.

"Gentlemen, this is a special meeting of your elected representatives. You are delaying our meeting. Please leave."

"Nope," the standing man spoke and the others nodded agreement. "We want to hear any plans you may have about our library. We're listening…"

Spokes templed his fingers in what he thought a conciliatory fashion. "We appreciate your interest in that facility. It's but one of the topics we are considering today."

"Well, go ahead!"

"Your name, sir, since you seem to be the spokesman."

"Charley Moss. We are all," he inclined his head, "daily users of that fine library."

"Okay, Mr. Moss. Here's my deal. All of you sit quietly, without interrupting our discussions *or*…"

Moss bristled. "Or what?"

Spokes pointed his finger. "Or I'll call the police and have you forcibly removed and arrested."

"Arrested on whut charges?" Charley demanded.

He looked at his companions' changed expressions at the word 'arrest.'

"Oh, all right. We'll be quiet." Rolling his eyes, he took his seat.

"We were about to examine the Police report," Spokes said, "if anyone forgot."

With that, he thumbed his notes. "The Police

got the 911 call from the Library at 2:45 p.m. and dispatched two patrol cars. On arrival at 2:52 p.m., the officers reported the situation inside the Library. The Captain and four more officers were dispatched to the Library, conferring with the chief librarian…"

"Whoa!" Charley raised his hand. "Her title is Library Director, not chief librarian."

Spokes ignored the interruption, continuing "at 3:00 p.m., immediately establishing traffic control points outside the Library on Water Street. Later, after the situation had been resolved, the Captain ordered the traffic officers back to the station at 6:00 p.m. End of mission. Any questions about the Police reaction?"

No hands were raised. Spokes punched a fist in the air for emphasis. "Good job, Police!"

Next he picked up the Fire Captain's report and thumbed through it. "The 911 at 2:45 p.m. was the common summons to both the Police and Fire. The Fire Captain ordered the Fire Rescue Team to respond and they arrived at the Library at 2:55 p.m.. Once they learned the victim's location and problem, they began trying to extricate an elderly man from the toilet in which his elbow cast was caught. Using an electric saw, they broke away the cast and eventually got the man out of the toilet."

Spokes couldn't resist a grin. "Next time you're hung up in a toilet bowl, you now know exactly who to call for help." Everyone at the table joined the laughter. The frowning, elderly men sitting against the wall were silent.

"To continue with the Fire report, the victim, a seventy-nine year old male, was conscious and lucid during the entire rescue. They put him on a stretcher and delivered him to the hospital at 3:49 p.m.. The hospital staff replaced the victim's elbow cast, later released him at 6:00 p.m.

"Questions or comments about the Fire Rescue effort?"

One of the council members spoke. "The team seems to have exactly the right equipment onboard their vehicle. Very professional, I'd say."

"Any other comments?"

"Our last report to review is that of the chief librarian...I mean, the Library Director," Spokes watched Charley Moss for a reaction.

"As said previously, the Library made the 911 call at 2:45 p.m.. Police and Fire responded quickly, as their reports indicated.

"The Library report is the most interesting of the three. It says the victim, a Mr. Charles Mass... the last name is illegible... of a Carrville address, was in the gent's restroom, using the toilet.

"Here's the amusing part. While flushing the toilet, the man sneezed so hard his false teeth went down the tube. Panicky, he jammed his arm into the toilet to rescue the teeth. Since that particular elbow was encased in a large plaster cast, the elbow stuck in the toilet bend and he was unable to get it--or his false teeth--out."

By now, all the council members were hooting with amusement.

"Any questions, comments?"

Angry, Charley Moss stood up.

"If you fine gentlemen are through cackling, that victim was me! I was the guy rescued from that toilet! And I'm here to tell you that the Library Director and her staff deserve some kinda' recognition for quickly getting me the help I needed!

"And let me tell you something else. The Police and Rescue Team were great. They performed in an emergency just like they trained and practiced. Those little ole librarians are not prepared or trained for emergencies. But they came through! Did the right things at the right time!

"Laugh at my predicament all you like, but don't overlook our fine, all purpose Library. You should send it an official commendation or sumthin'!"

Charley's companions rose and patted him on the shoulder as they filed out.

Suddenly the council members all stood and began applauding, regretting their earlier laughter.

Spokes called out to the departing old men, "Come again at any time! We value your input!"

Amy sat at her laptop, doing her nails, as the staff came through the back door, nodding and taking cups of coffee back to their own areas. Lara arrived last, in fancy jeans and boots.

"Want the good news first or the bad?" Amy asked.

Sighing, Lara sat down opposite her with fresh coffee. "Bad, unless there's too much of it."

"Harry, the only male of our library den, called earlier from Austin. He's decided to resign and start school at UT."

Lara peered into her coffee laconically. "We've been getting along without him for almost a month now. We'll hire a newbie and bring her or him up right.

"That the extent of the bad?"

"Not quite, Boss," Amy refilled her cup. "Angie, our yodeling teacher, has a sore throat so her class is cancelled. She'll tell us when she's recovered enough to resume. There were only four students in her class and we've notified them already."

"If that Harold doesn't buy you a ten pound box of chocolates, I will! You're a gem, Amy!"

Amy giggled. "Thanks, but Harold's comatose until after the football season. After my next tidbit, you may want to shoot the messenger. Remember the strange guy with the monocle?"

"The one who wants to reserve the Conference Room?"

"That's him, Mr. Donitz, by name. He's coming in at ten to deliver his application for use of the room."

"Fine," Lara's mind was elsewhere, wondering if Dan would show up today at the library. "I'll see Mr. Donitz whenever he shows. Sit in, if you've the time."

In the kitchen, Clarice was doing the weekly

clean-out of the refrigerator where employee lunches were stored.

"These pickles gotta go," she held the jar over the trash can. "They've turned grey instead of green. And this feta cheese," she held up another mildewed item.

Eugenia wandered into the kitchen. "What's that smell?"

"This cheese." Clarice dropped the offending articles into the trash. "Reminds me," she brightened, "of the saga of the widow with the great memory who outlived four husbands."

Grinning, Eugenia sat down. "Let's hear it."

Clarice held up one finger. "The first was a banker." She added a second upright finger. "The second, a musician." Another finger appeared. "Her third husband was a preacher and the fourth," another finger, "a mortician."

Dutifully, Eugenia asked, "Four husbands! How could she possibly remember each of their occupations for so long?"

Clarice wiggled with pride, delivering the punch line. "That's easy, the widow replied:

> *"One for the money,*
> *Two for the show,*
> *Three to make ready...,*

Laughing, they finished the rhyme together.

> *And four to go!"*

Upstairs, Lara, Doris and Donitz sat in Lara's office.

"Thank you for seeing me." From a black leather briefcase, he extracted papers which he handed Lara.

"My chapter's application for use of your conference room, Madame."

Doris scooted her chair over so she and Lara could read the application together.

A minute passed before Lara spoke. "I see you've already signed the application. Does that mean you understand and will fully comply with our Library rules?"

Grimacing, Donitz touched his necktie, then the monocle. "Yes."

Doris and Lara exchanged looks, before Doris half-nodded her head in encouragement.

"Just to review, Mr. Donitz, the rules to which you're agreeing. No smoking. No loud noises or parties which might disturb our patrons."

Donitz nodded twice.

"No consumption of food or beverages in the room or anywhere within the library."

He spoke a single word. "Agree."

After a moment, he held up a hand. "If our chapter meeting runs beyond normal library hours, may we remain until our business is completed?"

Doris and Lara exchanged head-shakes before Lara answered. "No, Mr. Donitz. You must observe our library hours, just like everyone else.

"Any other questions?"

"May we use the conference room for the first time next Tuesday from 10:00 a.m. until one?"

Lara made a note. "Consider it done, Mr. Donitz. We'll see you and your group then."

Smiling, Donitz headed out the office. As he turned to wave goodbye to Lara and Doris, he collided with Dan Roberts in the narrow hallway.

Roberts watched the other man leave, then grinned at Doris and Lara. "No need to call Fire and Rescue, ladies! I'm fine!"

They laughed at his joke. "Good morning," they repeated in unison.

"I'm here to ask you ladies to join me for lunch," he checked his fitbit. "It's already 11:30."

Doris objected. "Rod's coming for me at 12:00." Nudging Lara, she added, "I believe our Library Director's calendar may be free."

Lara was already shaking her head. "I must decline your kind offer, sir. I'm hosting the Brown Bag Book Club discussion at noon. We're discussing 'Pride and Prejudice.' You're welcome to join us."

After declining the invitation, Dan departed. Doris turned, looking Lara in the eye. "Notice anything strange?"

"What?"

"I think those two men know each other."

EIGHT

Shifting uncomfortably in a child's chair and surrounded by 4-6 year olds, Charley Moss glowed. He had been reading "Scooby Doo in the Forest" to the youngsters. From their apt faces, they enjoyed the tale as much as Charley.

Amy nodded at Charley as she left the reading room, giving him a high sign. She headed for the staff coffee room.

Seated there, Susan looked up and whistled. "Keen togs, girl! That studio skirt looks great on you!"

Sighing, Amy sat down with a thank-you. "I seriously need my C-cube this morning."

"What's that? If alcoholic, sign me up!"

"A cup of contemplative coffee equals C-cube. Unless we get a quick replacement for Harry, Eugenia and I won't be having many coffee breaks."

"Has the job even been announced?"

"Don't know, but I'll ask Doris at lunch. Ever notice how the work seems to increase as the holidays approach?"

"Yeah, and did you hear about that new bunch who'll start using our conference room?"

"Tell me."

"It's a bunch of history fanatics discussing medieval times in Germany."

"God save us. Going to happy hour after work?"

Susan gave a higher sign than she'd given Charley in the reading room. "The good news is that good ole Charley seems to enjoy reading to the kids on Wednesday. That's a help."

"Don't be late for happy hour! We need plenty of time to dissect that new 'Dan the Man' guy I keep hearing about."

"Dissect or disrobe?"

"Better not disrobe him within hearing of the Boss. I think she likes him."

Dan returned to the library before closing and repeated an invitation for dinner to Lara. Later, at her apartment door, he brandished a bouquet of roses and handily gained admittance.

"The classic greeting is 'You shouldn't have,'" she joked, taking the flowers.

"I hope," he responded, "these flowers announce this as an unofficial, non-business visit."

Ignoring his look, she turned hostess. "Beer, wine or bourbon?"

He settled on the sofa she pointed at. "Whatever you're having will be fine."

He looked about the room, noting overflowing bookcases, the usual TV and stereo. "Nice place. No room mate?"

"Don't you listen to my staff? I'm irascible."

"They're all afraid to talk to me," he countered. "You've got them thoroughly cowed, or maybe cowboy'd.

"But not me," he opened a folder of papers as she handed him a beer and sat beside him. "I'd like to insert a quick mention of 4-H business."

At her amused look, he continued. "Here's the schedule John Schoolfield, of the Carr County 4-Hers, and I worked out, if it meets your approval. I bring my bunch to your library on Saturday, from 10.00 a.m. until noon. On Sunday, I bring his 4-Hers at the same time.

"Here's our program for those two days: familiarization with library facilities, the computer terminals and how to operate them. Next, the use of the book inventory data base. Finally, each individual completes an application for a free library card."

Lara sipped her Coors. "Specifically, where does all this take place during a typically busy week?

"Well," he loosened the necktie selected especially for tonight, "I walk them through the floors, pointing out the arrangement of the stacks, and the equipment. Then we come down to floor two, gather around separate terminals and explain and demonstrate logging-in, and how to use Google and a bit of the menu."

Lara held up a finger "You're able to 'explain and demonstrate,' as you call the use of the terminals? You must be quite handy around the ranch, or wherever you call home."

"Lara," he leaned closer, "I'm anxious to illustrate my other talents to you...like cooking."

"Wow," she fended him off with a bowl of peanuts. "That's impressive for a cowboy. Is that what you really do for a living?"

An hour of give-and-take personal information passed so quickly, Lara caught her breath. "I neglected getting you another beer!"

Dan checked his watch. "I'd clean forgotten the time. Maybe we should go now for dinner before it gets any later. I thought of Margaritas, is that okay?"

On her way to the kitchen with the empties, she turned. "Somewhere else, please. That's where my staff always goes for Happy Hour.

"Immediately after they spotted us there" she splayed her hands, "the rumor would be that we are 'keeping company' as they said in the fifties..."

He helped her into a hoodie, whispering in her ear. "That's a crime for library science majors?"

"No, but then the next rumor would be that we're... Who knows what?"

"Let's keep them guessing," he suggested, opening the pickup door.

"Speaking of guessing," Lara settled into the passenger seat. "I'm guessing you know that monocled gentleman you ran into outside my office today?"

"Never seen him before," Dan cleared his throat and closed her door.

NINE

"Kin I come in?" Charley knocked on the glass window of the staff coffee room.

Clarice sat alone at the small table, trying to cool a hot coffee cup. She waved him in. "You've never asked before, Charley. You can come in if you promise not to sneeze your teeth out again. By the way, how did you clean those babies after you retrieved them from the toilet?"

"Soaked 'em in bleach, then scrubbed them with a brush. Now kin I come in?"

Her eyes lit up when she saw what he carried. "Are those chocolate donuts, Charley? Come, sit here beside me with those delicious little beauties."

"Kin I have a cup of coffee?" He asked before sitting down, carefully placing the donuts next to himself.

"Help yourself, but don't bang the clean cups. Do I have to plead for a donut, Charley? You're up to something, bringing us a dozen chocolates. What do ya' want?"

He smoothed his trademark red bandana. "Jest came by to chat with the lady who knows this ole library better'n anybody. She looks pretty dressy today in tight jeans and Nikes."

Despite the complement, Clarice didn't interrupt the first bite of her donut. "Thanks for the treat, Charley," as she finished it. "Now, let's lay our cards face-up. What is it you're after?"

Charley scooted his chair closer to hers. "It's that Conference Room upstairs. The one where we had the party last Christmas?"

Realizing his purpose, she confidently hooked another donut. "So?"

"Why all the changes being made to that room? That's one of the sure places us financial wizards sometimes can go for an uninterrupted snooze. Now there's a crew of workers up there hanging blinds on all the winders, even putting a lock on the door!

"What's going on, Miss Clarice?"

Clarice shrugged. "Might have somethin' to do with the new 4-H classes goin' in up there. Ask my boss…or that cowboy who keeps comin' to see her."

Charley was piqued. "4-Hers need window shades and a lock on the door? No more than a hog needs spurs!"

He scooped up the remaining donuts and fled.

"Guess it's up to ole Charley to find out what's happening up there to our comfortable snooze room. Me and my boys will find out, for sure!"

Meanwhile in the ladies' room, Susan and Amy stood at the mirror replenishing lipstick and combing hair. Amy looked over her shoulder at the toilet booths. All the doors were open.

"Guess we're alone and can talk. What's wrong with Lara? She acts like she's kinda taken with that Dan Roberts."

"Why not? She deserves a life outside these library shelves, doesn't she? I heard she was seen with that guy at Si-Si's, having pizza and mooning each other last night."

"That could be a game-changer! What if she went crazy, got married and left us?"

"What's on today, Doris?" Lara, the second person through the back door of the library today, wore skinny jeans and a colorful peasant blouse.

"Lookin' cool, Boss! Looks like you had your hair frosted. That means we can expect a visit from that cute Mr. Right today?"

Lara ignored the question, lowering her head as if concentrating on the daily schedule. "Thought we'd have a quick meeting at 8:00 and I'll introduce Ceci, our brand-new acquisition from the History Center next door."

Doris applauded. "That's great! You were quick to find us a replacement for Harry. I've met Ceci a time or two. I think she'll be a good fit in our crew."

Doris bent down to straighten a hose. "By the way, we missed you at Happy Hour last night."

"Ahh," Lara smiled shyly. "Well, Mr. Roberts and I were going over the plans for those 4-Hers using the library next Saturday and Sunday. I'd better cover that at our meeting, too."

Once everyone was settled around the table with a cup of coffee, Lara introduced Ceci. "We're lucky to steal Ceci Garcia from the History Center where she was part time. Welcome, Ceci, to the best multi-function staff and library in Texas, maybe the whole country!"

They put down coffee cups long enough to add to Lara's applause.

"Susan, would you please show Ceci around today, give her the grand tour to include a wall locker and get her started on re-shelving books from the carts?"

Susan spoke up. "Sure, but who's taking my place on the playground this morning?"

"I'll do that," Lara replied. "Now, let me tell you about the 4-Hers visiting us Saturday and Sunday from 10:00 'til noon. There will be two large 4-H groups here, one from Carr County, the other from Kandall County. We'll have to limit regular patron use of our on-line terminals for an hour both days.

Doris nodded and made a note.

A few miles away, the subject was also the 4-H visit on Saturday and Sunday. Dan had gathered the Kandall County chapter for a discussion of their individual projects at the Ag Barn east of town on route 27.

After individual presentations and discussions

about their projects, he began describing the library visit the next Saturday. On a large blackboard he listed his topics.

"Clothing," he began. "I want everyone to wear a clean 4-H jacket that day. It shows pride in our chapter if we look neat among all those city and library folks we'll see. Bring a pad and pen to take notes, just as you did today.

"Everyone bring a brown bag containing at least one sandwich and fruit. The library will provide us bottled water. Do not bring sodas, candy or such. This is going to be a healthy outing. After lunch we'll return here to the Ag Barn for your rides back home.

"Transportation. The library parking space is limited so I've hired a van to meet us here at 9:30, Saturday, and take us to the library. Be here and on the bus with your brown bag by 9:55, 'cause that's when we're leaving for the library. If you miss the bus, you'll be counted absent for a chapter meeting.

"After this visit, you'll be able to use the library terminals to find all kinds of information for your projects. You'll also be able to find specific books in the stacks, check them out using your new library card and take them home to read and study.

"I needn't remind you that if you lose or don't return a book on time, the library will charge you a fee. If you have to pay several fees, the library may cancel your card or deny your use of the computers.

"The library has lots of useful classes and services. You should try several of them. Use of the library puts us on a par with high school and university students living in town.

"Questions?"

Their enthusiasm--as evinced by the number of hands in the air--cheered Dan as he answered questions.

'That enticing Library Director will be as pleased by them as I am,' he thought as the program ended and everyone left to take the habitual sprint around the half-mile track which ended each chapter meeting.

"Ladies get a two minute head start!" he reminded the runners, then rang the cow bell to begin the run.

Later, as he started home in his pickup, Dan said aloud, "Wish I could please Lara as easily as I did those kids."

As usual Doris met Lara at the *Mr.Coffee* machine, but this time with a dour look. "After you hear the news," Doris sighed, "you may want to turn around and go back home."

"What's wrong? Bad date last night?"

Doris held up one finger. "First, the refrigerator in our kitchen went to Kenmore heaven last night, leaving defrosted mess all over the floor."

She held up a second finger. "Then our connection with the computer main frame failed but the IT folks are working to restore it."

A third finger appeared. "We found one of Charley's buddies asleep in the Conference Room. He slept the whole night there, unnoticed!"

Anticipating Lara's question, Doris fidgeted with her un-ringed finger. "Yes, Ma'm. We took away his library card and privileges. Our outstanding do-it-all lady, Clarice, already is working on the kitchen mess."

Lara sat down with a coffee and patted Doris on the shoulder. "What's that old expression about feces happening? You're doing great, Doris. If I can scrounge the money, you and Clarice deserve step increases."

This caused another wrinkle to Doris' forehead. "Speaking of money, where did we get the extra funds for those changes to the Conference Room?"

Lara blew on her hot coffee. "Would you believe it? That funny old Mr. Donitz paid for the changes himself since the upgrades are for the room he wants to begin using."

As they finished their coffee and walked to the reference desk, a fire alarm began screeching somewhere in the building.

"Fire alarm!" Doris whooped. "Oh, Lord! What next?"

"Fire alarm!" Lara repeated, motioning Amy at the checkout desk to open the two front doors.

"Everybody out!" Lara ordered the startled patrons, pointing to the open doors. "Assemble in the parking lot!"

As soon as she spoke, fire trucks could be heard clearing a noisy path down Main and Water Streets toward the library.

"Susan!" Lara pointed, "check the basement to make sure everyone is out. I'll check the third floor."

"No, I'll do the third," Doris objected. "You stay here on the second to meet the firemen."

"Deal! But where's the fire?"

Within minutes, the firemen had located the source of the alarm. From the third floor men's room, they hustled a frightened elderly man.

One of the firemen holding the man, grinned in relief "He was smoking a cigar in the men's room and the detector went off!"

The fire captain pointed. "You, get his ID. Tom," he pointed at another fireman, "double check all floors and rooms to make sure they're clear."

He nodded at Lara. "You'll get a copy of our report tomorrow. Looks like we're done here, as soon as all areas are cleared."

Lara's normal calm returned. "Thank you, Captain, for your marvelously quick response."

Doris pointed at the man still being held by two firemen. "What about him?"

"Open flame in a public building is at least a misdemeanor," the Captain said. "We're taking him with us."

Two reporters and a photographer cornered Lara. "Interview and photograph our Fire Captain instead of me!" she urged. "He and his men deserve all the credit! Go talk to him!"

"Think we can close early today, Boss? It's been a bummer so far."

Lara grinned at Susan and Eugenia. "I know you're kidding. This afternoon we host the Adult Book Club from 2:00 to 4:00."

Ceci Garcia touched Doris by the arm. "Is it always like this?"

Doris grinned at the library's newest member. "Pretty much! Sometimes, it's even worse! Wait until next Halloween!"

TEN

"Everything is goin' to be alright
So be my guest tonite"

Lara hummed the old tune on her way to work Friday morning.

"WHOA!" She suddenly realized what the words suggested.

"No way! I'm not inviting that guy anywhere! What came over me?"

She checked the rear view mirror a third time to make sure her hair was perfect. She'd spend a whole half hour making it curly-curly in the bathroom mirror.

Glancing at the vacant passenger seat beside her, she exclaimed again, "What's come over me?" The seat held a hamper of still-warm cookies covered by a clean dish towel.

Last night she'd baked four dozen to bring to work today for the library staff. A few might be left over for the 4-Hers arriving at 10:00 a.m.?

Did Dan like cookies? Her mind wandered and

she had to brake suddenly to avoid nudging the SUV ahead of her.

Instinctively she pulled into the library parking area, stopped and angled the mirror for a full face appraisal.

"What's wrong with you, Library Director? Shape up!"

Doris stared at her as she entered the coffee room. "Wow! You look like you just stepped off a *Mademoiselle* cover! Lovely studio dress! Black stilettos!"

"Oh, I get it! The 4-Hers are coming today!"

"Well, you look marvelous, Boss. He'll be eating out of your hand by 10:05!"

Lara dead-panned. "I don't know what you're going on about. Just another Monday at the old public library."

Doris sniffed at the hamper Lara set on the table. "I detect fresh, homemade cookies! That settles it! You're in love!"

Making a face at her friend, Lara stomped out of the room. Over her shoulder, she called, "The cookies are for us! I'm going out to check the playground. Heard the slide was muddy."

Doris chuckled. "In stilettos?"

By 10:00 a.m. Lara had visited both the beginner water color class and the social crafters in the basement. She stood near the reception desk, half-expecting that the 4-Hers wouldn't show or be late arrivals.

Suddenly a van pulled into the front driveway and a gang of youths wearing green 4-H jackets came through the front doors, led by Dan Roberts.

"Lafayette! We're here!" Roberts made a little bow. "May we use the Young Adult reading room as home base for the tour?"

After the youths were settled and quieted, Dan motioned Lara inside.

"This is Miss Beyer," he introduced her, "who is both Library Director and the kind lady designing our visit today." He led the 4-Hers' applause.

"This is a first. We are the first 4-H Chapter invited here to learn how we can use these superb facilities and equipment to advance our individual projects. Not only that, we will learn how to research library archives, just like college students.

"By raised hands, show Miss Beyer how many of you intend to go to college."

The majority of the youths raised a hand.

"Welcome to our library," Lara spoke. "Tell me, what are some of the areas in which you plan to major in college?"

"Animal husbandry," were several responses.

"Range management."

"Business administration."

"Kinetics."

"Medicine."

"Home economics."

"Education."

There were so many answers, she grinned at their fervor and diversity.

"That's splendid. This library is one of your best sources for research and study in each of those fields. You're in exactly the right place this morning. We're happy to have you here!"

She stood aside as Dan reiterated the areas and equipment the 4-Hers would see that morning. "With your permission, I'll start them out on this floor," he whispered.

She touched his arm. "Just a suggestion. Since we're here with all the terminals, why don't we start here instead of upstairs? Doris and Amy are primed to demonstrate to them how to enter, log-on and search for material. Our other patrons are temporarily barred from using these terminals."

She looked inquiringly at Dan, nodding his head with each of her changes.

"Let's do it, Library Director!" He was so enthusiastic that he caught her hand.

With that, Doris and Amy began demonstrating how to use the on-line terminals. Lara and Dan conferred how to rearrange the schedule they had just jumbled. "We can still complete on time," they said, looking at the penciled changes.

Upstairs, Lara walked the group through the book stacks, pointing out the different sections: fiction, non-fiction, Texana, large print, periodicals and encyclopedias.

At a terminal enabling queries of library

acquisitions, she demonstrated how to define a specific subject, title or author. Several 4-Hers performed searches for their personal projects. Whooping with success, they pointed out their findings. Others quickly took their places at the terminals.

"Now, note the location of the book you just searched for, take down its call number and find it in the stacks." Several others volunteered to perform similar tasks.

In the third floor Conference Room, she and Dan passed out cookies and applications for individual library cards. "Take your completed cards to the check-out desk downstairs and give them to Susan or Eugenia. Your laminated cards will be mailed to the address you wrote on your application, so make sure you write it correctly."

In one corner of the room sat Charley Moss, contentedly munching a cookie with the 4-Hrs. "Didn't know you were a 4-H advocate, Charley," Dan said.

"I came here to see how those new window shades and the locked door were being used by these kids. They ain't. Those changes to the Conference Room are mighty mysterious but I'll figure it out. Who uses the room next?"

"Don't know," Dan said. "Check with Doris, she'll know."

Dan shifted his attention to Lara, still doling out applications and cookies. "If we're out of here by noon," he said, "I'm coming back this evening after I deliver my young charges to the Ag Barn."

She raised her eyebrows. "Why?"

"To treat you to a well-deserved dinner at the best place in town. Seven o'clock?"

At her pensive look, he added, "Please?"

The entire staff, minus Lara, sat in the lunch room, chatting, after the 4-H tour.

"He's, hot, hot," Eugenia contributed, to several nods. Everyone knew who she meant.

Susan pouted. "Did you notice? They were never more than three feet apart."

"Yeah," Eugenia rubbed her forehead at the memory, "like they were joined at the hip or something. Or wanted to be."

Ceci, the newest member, smiled at their banter but was silent.

Doris cracked her knuckles before challenging the others. "You know what we should do, if we had a little intestinal fortitude?"

"She means guts," Susan explained. "What should we do, Doris?"

"Like at the Super Bowl. Fans bet on the final score and put the score they forecast into a pot."

Amy suddenly raised a hand. "And the person who guesses the closest score, wins the pot!"

"We could do that!" Eugenia twisted a loose lock of grey hair.

"There's no Super Bowl here," Amy objected. "What are we talking about?"

Doris rapped on the table. "If you want to play,

you write down the date you think something really significant will occur between Lara and that cowboy."

"Like their first kiss?" Ceci volunteered softly.

"No, and not their first date, either. I think they're already beyond that." Clarice opined.

Amy looked up from filing fingernails. "How about the date of their engagement? It'll be in the papers so we'd all know about it."

"What if they never get that far?" Clarice reheated her coffee.

"Pessimist!" Eugenia accused. "Of course they'll get that far! Can't you tell by the way they look at each other?"

Doris rapped on the table again. "We're getting nowhere. Let's vote on the event. I like the date of engagement best, optimist that I am.

"Who votes for the engagement date?"

Five hands went up, all except Clarice.

"They'll never get that far," she insisted. "Haven't you heard of a one-nighter followed by 'OMG! I'll never do that again?'"

"That sounds like a great tale, Clarice. Let's hear all the details at our Christmas party," Amy chuckled.

"Date of engagement wins," Doris insisted. "How much shall we each divvy up?"

Wistfully, Ceci said, "I can only afford ten bucks. New job and all," she shrugged.

"Ten sounds about right to me," Doris injected, pulling a large bank deposit envelope out of a drawer.

"Here's mine." She put a ten into the envelope and signed her name on the front of the envelope.

The others did the same, even Clarice, who put hers in last. "I'm still not convinced they'll get engaged but I'll go along."

She cackled. "Because I'm betting my 'never happen' entry takes the pot."

"Here," Susan passed out slips of paper and pencils. "Put the date you think they'll get engaged and your name on this slip, fold it and put it in the envelope."

"Don't tell or show anyone what date you wrote."

"Except me," Clarice repeated, scribbling on her note. "Never happen."

"Where do we keep the pot and our notes?"

"I'll lock it up with our 'paid library fees." Doris offered. "Nobody goes in there except me once a month to make a bank deposit. Any objections?"

There were none.

"Finally," Amy leaned forward and put her hand on the table. "Everyone must swear to keep this a secret. Nobody talks about this bet or the date each of us chose! Ever! Agreed?"

Five other hands clasped on the table.

ELEVEN

Dressed in his best snap-button western shirt and starched levis, Dan knocked on her door, juggling a small box of chocolates in one hand and flowers in the other.

"Punctual." She glanced approvingly at her watch as she opened the door and gestured him inside. "Just like our 10:00 appointment this morning."

She glanced at his hands. "Thank you for these lovely gifts."

Her voice changed timbre. "But no more, please," she chided, wondering again how he could afford them.

"Not from me," he protested. "These are in recognition of your splendid performance this morning. They are gifts from the thankful members of the Kandall County 4-H Chapter." He shrugged, "I had nothing to do with it."

She took his hat and they perched on the living room sofa. Smiling, they eyed each other a moment before she offered beer and peanuts.

"This exposes your Texas roots," he pointed at the beer label. "Lone Star."

"It's the best a poor librarian can offer," she kidded. "I had to steal from the coffee fund to afford it."

Her free hand was beside him and he grabbed it. "I'm very impressed," he looked at her steadily.

"I think you are a surprise, very much out of the normal library science, master's degree, mold. Are you happy here or do you secretly desire to be on an Austin committee, selecting acquisitions for all Texas libraries?"

She withdrew her hand with a tug and a rueful look. "You read palms! Please don't reveal my secret ambition!"

"Really?" he laughed.

"No, of course not," she giggled. "I'm simply playing your silly game."

"Whew," he breathed loudly. "You gave me a start!"

"No more games?" she suggested.

"Agree! No more games," he captured her hand again and looked at his watch.

"Shall we go now?"

"Never been here before," she said as they entered the restaurant. "What's this place?"

"Wrangler Steakhouse," he still held her hand. "Apropos, don't you think?"

After ordering drinks, they studied long menus. "Beef's best here," he said. "Lots of our best Herefords end up on these platters," he nodded at an adjoining table being served steaks.

"What does Mr. Cowboy recommend we eat at the Steakhouse?"

"Another drink," he predicted, "then a filet or ribeye, whichever you fancy."

"I didn't realize I was so hungry," she later wiped her mouth, pushing away her plate. "It was scrumptious."

"Sounds like a graduate student kind of word," he joked. "Now for coffee and their special carrot cake."

Much later they were back at her apartment. "I had a marvelous time tonight, Dan. Thank you. I'd ask you in for more coffee but I can't match that carrot cake. As you know, we have another 4-H session tomorrow. I've got be bright, early and ready for those kids.'"

"I'll be there." He attempted a hug.

She shied away. "But tomorrow's group is from Carr County, not yours."

Nodding ruefully, he grinned. "True, but I hope to see you. Be sure to wear something that goes with green."

She stood on the library steps to welcome the 4-Hers. The wait was short, as a van suddenly turned into the parking lot and discharged young women and men, all wearing green 4-H shirts.

Leading the youths was Dan.

"I thought you were kidding, about coming," she began. "Where's Mr. Schoolfield?"

"John had a flat tire, so he'll join us later. Since you

and I did the tour yesterday, I thought I could do it solo today. Allow you to catch up with your Director duties."

In a mock voice, she asked, "Sure you can handle it? Doris and Amy are available for the on-line terminal demos again. This smaller group today will get even more practice than your bunch yesterday."

"Thank you, thank you," he beamed. "I hope to see you, Doris and Amy for a moment before we leave at 12:00?"

"Sounds mysterious," she blinked. "Librarians are always available."

Dan led the Carr County 4-Hers over the identical tour taken by the Kandall County group the day before. Amy and Doris obliged by again demonstrating the use of the on-line computer terminals on the library main floor. As before, several young people sought information from the terminals to be used in their individual 4-H projects.

Dan led the group upstairs to the stacks, pointing out where types of material were located. Using information gained from their queries downstairs, several youths searched for specific books among the stacks.

In the Conference Room, everyone completed an application for a library card, to be returned to the check-out desk downstairs.

"Take care of your library card once you get it in

the mail. It enables you to use a library just like college students."

Downstairs, Dan held up his hand. "Remember how we decided to thank the librarians for their help? Who did you elect to be our spokesperson?"

"Marcia Gonzales," several called out as a young lady stepped forward to face Lara, Doris and Amy.

She grinned at the three librarians. "On behalf of our chapter, I thank you and your entire staff for permitting us to learn important lessons here today. We are certain to use those lessons not only in our 4-H projects, but later as college students."

With that she handed them each a green 4-H T-shirt embossed with their chapter name. Surprised by the gift, the three librarians looked at each other, hesitated, and began donning the green Tees.

"Thank you," the three said, almost in unison, grinning as they carefully pulled the shirts over hair-do's.

"We'll often wear them here," Lara pledged, "hoping to see all of you in our Library more often!"

"Thanks for your visit to the best little ole library in Texas!" Doris boasted, waving goodbye.

Meanwhile, John Schoolfield joined the crowd, adding his thanks. As the 4-Hers and Schoolfield trooped outside to the van, Dan hesitated beside Lara.

"Couldn't resist," he began, handing her a large bakery box. "It's one of those carrot cakes you seemed to enjoy last night. For you and your staff. Thank you!"

Looking relieved and sighing, he hurried outside to catch the departing van.

TWELVE

Tuesday began differently. The elderly readers of the *Journal* lined up outside the Conference Room upstairs instead of queuing to read the financial news at the reference table.

Charley Moss, among others, stood along the wall outside the Conference Room, dourly inspecting the silent members of the Donitz group as they entered, then closed and locked the room door behind them.

"Mighty suspicious looking characters," Charley began his critique of the half-dozen well-dressed strangers who walked by, ignoring their elderly adversaries.

Loudly, he tried the room's door knob. "Locked tighter than a banker's billfold," he announced.

"What are they doing in there, Charley? What kind of study group do they claim to be?" Roscoe Waller asked, trying the door knob with the same result.

"Doris, our reference lady, says they are studying ancient Germany when it was ruled by some old king named Frederick or something'."

"Why do they have to do it--whatever it is--in our

patch?" Anson Brown demanded, shaking his head. "We ought to complain to the Library Director! Kick them out! They look like radical-somethings to me!"

"Maybe we should report them to the Police," another greybeard commented.

"We need a spokesman...someone with clout...to help us, Charley."

"Who better than ourselves?" Charley countered. "We're all tax paying citizens."

After rattling the locked door again, the group slowly shuffled back down the stairs to take their usual places around the reference table.

On the way, Roscoe nudged Charley. "I think we should ask Doris for advice about complaining and demanding our room back. She always knows more about this place than us poor taxpayers."

As soon as they were seated, Donitz collared Bruno, his security officer. "Who were those ruffians in the hallway?"

"I don't know, sir, but I'll find out. They look like harmless old men. I assure you, sir, they have more to fear from us than the reverse."

"Have you conducted a thorough screen of this room?"

"Yes, sir. I did."

"Any discoveries?"

"Only some cut wires found in one corner. There was also refuse indicating someone has been sleeping in the room. Apparently, this room is not cleaned frequently."

Donitz nodded. "I'll add that to my complaint list that I intend to present to Madame Library Director."

"A woman, sir? I think a man would be more appropriate if we expect corrective action to be taken."

"Perhaps you are right. You have someone in mind, Bruno?"

"Yes, sir. I saw a tall man earnestly talking to that female director. He seemed to absorb her complete attention. I'll ask his name."

Turning his attention to his audience, Donitz thanked them for being on time, particularly at this new venue. "As we have discussed before, we are best hidden from public scrutiny if we are in plain sight. What better place than a public library?"

By the number of nodding heads, there was total agreement.

"Welcome to the twenty-first meeting of this chapter of the Order of Frederick 1, our revered King and Kaiser. The purpose of this meeting is to acquaint you with this new facility and assess its appropriateness for future meetings.

"As you have seen from our entrance here, there is a group of elderly patrons who appear upset by our presence.

"I assure you, Bruno will attend to this matter in his usual quiet, effective manner.

"A brief mention of this library's rules, some of which we will honor. No smoking here or loud talking that might be heard outside this room. There is also a rule against bringing in beverages and food, a rule we shall overlook as we desire, beginning today. Questions?"

A hand was raised.

"Yes?"

"Are we in communication with that representative at the civilian DNA-testing company mentioned at our last meeting?"

"Yes, we are. Further on the topic of communications, Bruno has screened this room and assures me that there are no hidden cameras or recording devices here. That reminds me of our individual oaths not to take notes or photographs here. It is equally important that we individually safeguard our discussions and intended actions."

He looked at each member in turn. "Disobedience would be a terrible mistake, both for you individually as well as for your families. Again, I ask by a show of hands that this is clearly understood by each of you."

Donitz paced the few steps in front of his rapt listeners, again staring at them and noting all hands raised.

"Very well, thank you," he smiled for the first time. "Now, for our short program for this meeting. Bruno's handing folios to those of you in seats one, three and five. One, three and five will share these folios with comrades in seats two, four and six. The folios contain a synopsis of the genetic backgrounds of three persons of interest to our order.

"Your purpose is to select the most likely candidate or candidates for further action in pursuit of our order's goal: the elimination of persons of direct lineage responsible for the death and defamation of our King and Kaiser, Frederick 1.

"You have one hour, beginning now, to make an assessment and recommendation with your seat partner. At our next meeting, we will conclude our research with recommendations for possible action."

In exactly one hour, the three annotated folios were collected by Bruno. During the interim he opened the large leather case he had carried inside. He lined the table with eight filled wine glasses and set-up the heraldic flag of their order.

They stood silently at the table, holding glasses until Donitz offered a loud toast:

"KOENIG UND KAISER ROTBART!"

After toasting King and Kaiser Rotbart (Red Beard, byname of Frederick 1) each man symbolically snapped the stem of his glass and handed the pieces to Bruno.

Charley and Anson Brown were at Doris's desk even before Donitz and company were out the front door. Charley nodded toward the Young Adult reading room. "Doris, kin Anson and me have a private word with ya' in there?"

She looked up, in the middle of a telephone conversation. "Just as soon as I'm free of this call," she mouthed.

Inside the reading room, Charley erupted. "We want to complain about those strangers who been up in our Conference Room," Charley began. Anson accompanied the narrative with emphatic nods.

"Whose Conference Room, Charley?"

"Well... it's yours, Doris, as everybody--except those strangers--knows."

Doris drew a breath. "Okay, Charley. What's your gripe about a group of individuals reserving and using the Conference Room. They're patrons, just like you and Anson."

Charley licked his lips. "First of all, why is there a lock on that door? It's never had a lock before these strangers came. What are they doing in there that's so secret, I want to know."

Anson interrupted. "Don't forgit about the gulping and breaking glass noises."

"I ain't forgetting, Anson, I was just going to mention that.

"There's no smoking or drinking or eating allowed in there, right, Doris?"

She heaved a sigh. Complaints from the 'Wall Street Snorers' as she called them, were no novelty.

"Is that all you've got?" She wrinkled her nose.

"They might be terrorists, planning on blowing up our library!" Charley exploded. "You ain't concerned?"

Doris complacent grin was his answer,

Angry, Charley stalked out of the room. "We ain't through! You jest sit back and shut your eyes! We're going to find real evidence!"

"Then you'll be sorry!" Anson added, slamming the door.

THIRTEEN

Surprising herself, Lara invited Dan to her apartment for supper that evening. Wearing his best stockman's jacket and trousers, he stood at her door with another bouquet.

"You've got to quit bringing flowers!" She exclaimed, more pleased than ever. "What will my neighbors think?"

"That you're graciously inviting a starving cowboy to a home-cooked meal." He rolled his eyes. "What else?"

"Not knowing what we're having, I brought a bottle of cheap red as well," he produced a bottle from behind his back.

"Clairvoyant, aren't you? That's perfect for my homemade *Chef Boyardee* and salad. Graduate school was short on fine cooking."

Once back on the couch, they clinked chilled beer bottles and grinned at each other. "How was work today?"

"Fine," Lara tucked long legs under her. "Except this was the first time we were visited by a strange

German historical group who used our Conference Room for a couple hours."

"I know," Dan took an offered pretzel. "For some reason I was accosted this afternoon by a Mr. Donitz of that same bunch."

"I thought you didn't know him?"

He answered warily. "I didn't, before today. He came to me with some complaints he should have made directly to you or someone at the library."

"Spaghetti's boiling!" she interrupted, leaping up and running to the kitchen. "Even grad students recognize that signal! Time to eat! Uncork that fabulous red wine and sit down!"

After mopping up spaghetti sauce with what was left of the thick crusty bread, Lara sat back and re-tucked her legs. "Now, let's hear your report, secret agent of this mysterious cabal."

"I didn't know the man until this morning. He walked up to the table where John and I were having breakfast. We had decided to get together and review our plans for our library visits next weekend.

"This Donitz character sat down and requested that I repeat to you his complaints about their visit yesterday. I am *not* his secret agent or whatever that implies."

"Did he buy your breakfast?"

Despite his tan, Dan blushed. "He did, for both of us. Was I supposed to say 'No, thank you. Get away?'"

Lara got up. "Coffee? I'm having some."

"Sure, thanks. By the way, your spaghetti

was outstanding. I'd have never known it wasn't homemade."

"Not only are you a secret agent, you're a great fibber, too. What else did he say?"

"He said the room was untidy. There were a few loose electric wires about and someone had been sleeping in the room."

Lara widened her eyes. "Thanks. I'll take care of that. What else?"

"His major gripe was that a group of 'elderly men,' as he called them, were in the hall outside the Conference Room, making angry remarks and gestures at them. Once his group was inside the room, several of the men outside rattled the locked door, trying to get in."

Lara sighed. "Sounds like Charley and his buddies. They think that room belongs to them. I'll change their thinking about that notion. Anything else?"

"He said to thank you and your staff for allowing them to meet there and asked for a similar reservation next month, same time."

Dan wiped his forehead with his napkin. "I'm embarrassed to be in this position, asking and reporting things on his behalf. I really have no personal interest in that group, whatever it is.

"Especially after being invited here for a superb supper with you. Can I be forgiven before we go farther?"

She smiled. "I forgive you. What might going *further* entail?"

"Okay, I meant further...to meet my mother at our place near Comfort?"

This time he was allowed a doorway goodbye kiss-on-the-cheek.

The next morning Amy was the first to open up and turn-on *Mr. Coffee*. "Good morning!" was her happy greeting to Lara.

"Happy Monday!" she repeated, resplendent in embellished jeans and red drape-front top. "Have some coffee!"

"Good morning to you, bright and cheerful partner! Why up so early on a Monday?"

"A beautiful day, don't you think? What a great day to have our dedication ceremony!"

Lara sat down with her coffee, trying to catch up. "What ceremony?"

"Don't you remember? The dedication of that toilet in the men's room where Charley baptized his false teeth!"

Without pausing, Amy rolled out a diagram. "Here's what I'm having the engravers put on a small metal plaque to place over the toilet. If you don't like the words, we'll change them before our ceremony this evening after we close the library."

"Oh!" Lara's surprise changed to understanding. "The toilet caper last week? We thought a small ceremony would be put that strange event behind us and be an excuse to celebrate?"

"Yeah, Boss, that's it." Amy unrolled the paper exposing her words for the plaque:

In Solemn Memory of Charley's Toilet Caper Here September 7, 2018

"My only question--if you approve the wording--should we invite Charley to the ceremony or would it be too embarrassing for him? What if, in the excitement, he sneezed his choppers into the crapper a second time?"

"Good question," Lara, giggling, poured another coffee. "First, tell me what other wonders you have planned for this 'solemn ceremony.'"

"We close the library at the normal time and get our staff in the men's john that Charley made famous. You say a few dedicatory words, we take a photo...I think everyone will want a copy, don't you? Then we have a little champagne and go to Margaritas for our usual happy hour."

"Quite a plan, Amy! Congrats. How do we afford the champagne?"

Amy glowed. "No problem! A magnum of the stuff was given me last Christmas which I now donate to forgetfulness of Charley's episode!"

Clarice arrived as Amy unfolded her plan. "Sounds great! Maybe we should all wear a red bandana like Charley? How did you plan to serve the bubbly?"

"We get some paper cups from the *Dollar Store*,"

Amy answered. "And I've got some red fabric we can cut into bandanas. How's that?"

"No way the paper cups!" Clarice intoned. "There are lots of juice tumblers in the kitchen. I'll wash them and get them upstairs. This is going to be fun!"

"Who's going to take the photo?" Lara asked. "We want everyone in it."

"I'll ask Jerry from the *Daily Reporter* to show up for a quick photo. He won't have to stay but a minute. Maybe, he'll even write an article about it."

"No thanks to an article," Lara objected. "Something about us in the paper would cause another probe by those commissioners. We don't need that."

"Agreed," Amy said "So we're set to assemble in the--we hope--vacant men's room as soon as we get all our patrons out of the building at closing."

Clarice wondered, "How will Jerry, the photographer, get in and out?"

"I'll let him in and escort him out as soon as he's taken our photo," Amy volunteered. "And I'll ask him to print us seven copies."

On her way to the front, Clarice confided, "You know, this *is* a great little library, isn't it?"

"Yes, we are!" Lara and Amy shouted in unison.

FOURTEEN

Chuckling, two of the "Nodders' sat at a café table the next morning. Anson pushed the morning newspaper at Roscoe, pointing to a photograph on the front page.

"Hey, Roscoe! Bet you didn't know we're sitting here with a mighty famous person whose picture is on page one."

The newspaper was the *Daily Reporter*. A photo caption read:

LIBRARY HOLDS DEDICATION CEREMONY

The short accompanying news article explained that the library staff had installed a small plaque in the men's room where a patron caused an emergency requiring his recent extrication by the Fire Department's Emergency Rescue Team.

"The emergency was previously reported in the *Reporter* last Friday.

The commemorative plaque, centerpiece of yesterday's dedication ceremony, read 'In Solemn

Memory of Charley's Toilet Caper Here September 7, 2018."

Charley took his seat at the reference table and immediately grabbed the paper to see what was so funny.

"Damn!" he choked with rage. "Did they have to humiliate me agin?"

With that, he stalked off to the office of the Library Director to register a fiery complaint. Despite Lara's assurances that they had asked the photographer not to write a news story or publish the photo, Charley was still angry.

"Sit down and take a deep breath, Charley," Anson advised. "Remember your blood pressure."

"Yeah," Roscoe stood. "Let's get him out of here, Anson, and get us a cup of coffee somewhere."

"Good idea," Anson agreed and the two pulled Charley out the door.

Once seated in the nearest café, Anson easily redirected Charley's attention. "Ya' know when that strange group is coming back to use our Conference Room again?"

The others shook their heads.

"Well, they have the room reserved for Tuesday, from 10 in the morning until one. I say we should plan a grand surprise for them."

"Surprise?" Charley's interest almost crackled.

"Someway to get them kicked out of our library,

is what he means, Charley. Like…," Roscoe paused, "like them causing a commotion or something."

"How about sending them a pot of coffee with laxative in it? Make them all sick and run out."

"Maybe install a secret speaker and blast their talk all over the library?" Charley grinned. "What's so secret about what they do in there, anyway?"

"If they're doing somethin' illegal, we should tell the police. But we need evidence!"

"For sure, we could jimmy that new door lock so they can't keep us out again."

"Hell," Charley was jubilant. "Let's remove the door!"

Anson cautioned. "That's no good, we'd be blamed instead of them strangers."

"There must be somethin' we can do to keep them out."

Roscoe cracked his knuckles in frustration. "Let's think more about it, real hard."

"But keep it under our hat," Charley nodded, picking up the coffee check.

"No friendly greeting?" he asked as she opened her apartment door, steadily regarding him.

"Come in." Still not smiling, Lara pointed to the chair opposite the sofa where they usually sat. Two drinks were on the coffee table. One was half empty.

"What's this?" He sat in the appointed chair and lifted his glass toward her in toast.

"Beam and branch water." She sat on the sofa, lifting her own glass.

He noticed her half glass. "Looks like you're ahead of me."

She sipped her drink. "I had to prepare myself for what I'm about to say."

Surprised by her tone, his smile evaporated. "What is it?" He set down his untasted drink.

"Do you remember we agreed that there would be no games between us?"

Perplexed, he nodded.

"Yet I'm confused. You're enticing me into a game right now by an innocent appearing invitation to meet your mother."

He blinked, then smiled rigidly. "It's a simple, straightforward invitation, Lara. Not a game, I assure you."

"Hear me out!" she demanded. "So I'm invited to go home with you and meet your adoring dear mother. While there, she'll show me your baby pictures, maybe tiny bronzed shoes, your Boy Scout merit badges and we'll enjoy a delicious homemade meal.

"Right?"

At her question, Dan reached for his bourbon and water and took a sip. He attempted humor. "Looks like I may need this strengthened. Maybe even a double!"

Lara glared. "Thus softened up, I'm putty in your practiced hands. Vulnerable! Once back here you think you can jump my bones and spend the night."

Dan exploded. "Wrong! How could you think such a thing?"

"Wrong is right!" She jumped to her feet "It ain't going to happen, cowboy, or whatever you are!"

He struggled to his feet, shaking his head. "Does this sour mood have something to do with that strange Donitz guy?"

Her eyes flashed. "Yeah, that's your second game, isn't it? Why are you that strange man's patsy? Why did you relay his silly complaints to me instead of his telling me directly?"

"What's going on? Is he paying you? What's he got on you?"

Finishing his drink, Dan carefully placed the empty glass on the coffee table. "God, I'm disappointed in your attitude tonight. It was going to be perfect, meeting my mother and getting acquainted. That's out the window now. I sure didn't see this coming."

He grabbed his coat and opened the door. "Good night, Lara. I hope you're feeling better by morning."

"No need coming by the Library tomorrow to check out a few books," she slammed the door behind him.

Defiant yet miserable, Lara made a toasted cheese sandwich and another, stronger drink. Sprawled on the couch, she crooned along with a famous lament:

> *"Farewell, goodbye,*
> *Although I'll cry,*
> *Ain't that a shame?*

My tears fell like rain."

At the same time in Galveston, a meeting of the Order of Frederick 1 was convening in the Rosenberg Library on Sealy Street. The assemblage was small, only seven members others than Donitz and Bruno, the security officer.

"Usual inspection for devices?"

Bruno clicked his heels. "Yes, sir!"

"Come to order," Donitz announced after polishing and adjusting the monocle. "To those of you wondering why this venue was chosen for our meeting, I'll explain. Our recent experience is that the more public our meeting place, the more unnoticed we are. This meeting will further test that theory.

"I remind you of your individual oaths once you became members of the Order of Frederick 1. Our membership, our discussions and our methods are secret. You defy our rules at your considerable risk.

"Do all of you here acknowledge your oaths of secrecy to our order? If so, raise your hand in solemn testimony."

Quickly all hands were raised as Donitz strode before them.

Satisfied, Donitz nodded at Bruno. "Your report, please."

Already standing, Bruno stepped forward. "Sir, I have two folios passed to me for appropriate action. They are the records of two individuals inimical to the heritage of our King and Kaiser. These individuals are the result of DNA analysis tracing their ancestors to the time of our liege, King and Kaiser, Frederick 1.

"The first of these is a seventy-two year old male living in the Houston area. I easily found his address and followed him, planning appropriate action for several days. Unfortunately, he eventually led me to the Houston International Airport where he boarded a flight to Belize City, out of our jurisdiction. He purchased a one-way ticket and I forwarded his folio to our chapter in Belize for action."

The member in seat number three raised a hand. "What about his properties and home? If he returns here, he remains our problem, does he not?"

Bruno frowned at the questioner before answering. "He was a renter, placing his goods in storage. Our Belize chapter reports the man currently is making inquiries about purchasing a home in the Belmopan area."

There was another hand, alongside the first. "Does the Belize chapter acknowledge further responsibility for him?"

Bruno grinned. "Yes, it does."

"The matter seems settled. This individual is no longer our responsibility. Any more questions concerning this folio?"

Donitz nodded at Bruno. "Please proceed with the next case."

Bruno cleared his throat. "Folio two is that of an eighty year old man, originally an émigré from Northern Italy, thus of particular interest to our contact in the commercial firm performing DNA research."

"And to us," Donitz interrupted.

"The police investigation found an auto driver, our subject, was distracted, ran off the parkway, striking a tree," Bruno was solemn. "Medical analysis of the victim's body revealed a high rate of alcohol may have contributed to his fatal accident."

"Questions?" Donitz stood at the temporary rostrum. "Thank you for your reports, Security Officer. Now we will hear Professor Anton, author of his just published book, "Barbarossa, Enigma of the Holy Roman Empire."

"Copies of his book are available later for your purchase. I've asked the Professor to not only review his work but to read significant portions concerning our beloved sovereign, Frederick 1.

"Professor Anton," Donitz led the applause as he led the professor, formally dressed in black, to the podium.

FIFTEEN

She awoke the next morning with a headache and runny nose. "Great! I'm almost late to work!" She dressed hurriedly, grabbed the briefcase and ran outside to start her car.

Turning into the library parking lot, she slowed, eying a small group of women milling about the front door, some waving homemade signs.

Inside the back door, Doris silently handed her a cup of coffee. "You'll need this, Boss. Sit down and let me tell you about the crazies out front.

"We have several older women protesting a book that one of them checked-out which deeply offends them."

Lara tasted the hot coffee. "One of our books?"

"Yep, they are waving a copy of what they're calling a 'risque novel.' The title is *Fifty Shades of Grey*, checked out from us last year and never returned."

"What do they want?"

"They want the book removed from our shelves PLUS any others they term inappropriate,"

"Inappropriate to whom?"

"That they haven't explained in the brief confrontation I had with them a minute ago."

"I'd better go out and talk to them. Maybe get them to leave before the press arrives."

"Good luck with that! I'm going with you."

Outside Lara stared at the signs being waved in her face by three angry, well-dressed women.

"BAN FIFTY SHADES OF FILTH!"

"DRAIN THE LIBRARY!"

"CLEAN READING, CLEAR MINDS!"

"Are you the Library Director?" The woman with the first sign lowered it long enough for Lara to answer.

"And responsible for this despicable trash," she waved a copy of a book, "being available to the reading public--including innocent children?"

Lara took a deep breath, suddenly as feisty as she had been the previous evening with Dan.

"Yes! I'm Lara Beyer, director of this public library whose purpose is to provide information in printed and other forms to diverse groups of patrons, all of whom may not be seminarians. We are a PUBLIC library.

"Patrons may request that we obtain a particular title for individual and collective reading or research. We have over 700,000 books, periodicals, and videos for public use. We currently serve over 30,000 city and county patrons, most of whom are quite happy and never complain about our collections."

"Indecent books like this one," the leader waved the book again, "should be heaped up and burned!"

Another sign-bearer yelled, "If you won't protect your readers from smut, we'll find someone who will!"

Lara held up her own hand, angrier than ever. "Like all public libraries, we maintain the standards of the American Library Association. If you take issue with our library, I invite you to join me for a tour of our facilities to better understand what we do. You'll see we daily serve a large variety of patrons of all ages and interests.

"Perhaps you are unaware that we offer a variety of services and activities in addition to our collections. Today you can visit an adult book club meeting, a social crafters work group, attend exercises for better balance or a 'capture your family story' workshop.

"How may of you have a library card?"

Momentarily unaware, none acknowledged a card.

"Are you ready to begin a tour of our library right now or would you prefer coming back at a time more convenient to you? Just let me know when."

Again, her question caught them by surprise.

"I can't. We have a flower club luncheon," one frowned.

"And I have a dentist appointment at eleven."

A third lady held up both hands. "I've got to take a makeup exam to get my driver's license back."

The leader, her sign now drooping, was angry at her colleagues' flagging interest. She made a face at Lara. "You've not heard the last of this! My husband's a commissioner and he will be just as displeased as we are. You'll hear from us again. I'm writing a letter to the newspaper editor so the whole town knows of your negligent performance and attitude!"

As the women fled in all directions to their cars, Doris patted Lara's shoulder. "Great work, Boss! They're leaving and the press is not even in sight."

"That threat to tell her husband and write letters to the newspaper will keep me awake all night."

In addition to trying to blot that damn cowboy out of my mind at midnight, Lara thought to herself.

That evening Henry Bozeman held a beer can in one hand and a long-handled barbeque fork in the other. He moved them in unison as if directing the meeting of the next council of which he was--as he described himself--a prominent member.

His wife's angry voice redirected his thoughts. "Don't let those ribs burn like you did the last time, Henry!"

She slid a bowl of potato salad onto the outdoor table with a sigh and seated herself in front of her husband. "Let me tell you what a terrible time I had at the library today, confronting that rude woman who's in charge."

He sighed, turning several ribs over and wishing she'd brought him another beer.

"Are you listening, Henry?"

He flipped another rib. "Yes, dear."

"It was terrible," she repeated. "A group of us met at the library to protest a pornographic book we found there, available to any child with a library card. We told the chief librarian, a Miss Beyer--looks like a teenager herself--to remove the book and all others like it."

"What's the book about, dear?"

"A totally degenerate story about a wealthy control freak who seduces an innocent young college student, then enslaves her in his immoral sexual activities.

"We even had made signs to make clear our desires but she put us off with a grandiose description of the library's functions. I was highly irritated by her attitude as were the other ladies.

"Now, Henry, I want you to air this terrible menace to our youth at the next commission meeting. Not only must you demand a scourging of all inappropriate library books, I want you to withdraw that award the library is to receive for that peculiar toilet episode last week!"

Henry looked at his watch. "Can't this wait? It's cocktail time. Besides..." his tone changed to his most persuasive. "Didn't you ever sneak a read of a sultry chapter in *Forever Amber* when you were in grade school? Or *Fanny Hill*? They didn't seem to hurt you one little bit, did they?"

"Stop it, Henry! I'm ashamed of you! Now I want to make this clear. I'm depending on your help with those silly commissioners.

"Our group of ladies is sending a letter to the newspaper editor about that librarian's *laissez-faire,* irresponsible attitude.

"With our help, your directing the commission's action to withdraw that library commendation should be simple."

He crushed the empty beer can and tossed it into the trash.

She shouted "Henry, did you hear a word I said?"

SIXTEEN

The next morning the back door opened before she reached it. Doris offered Lara a cup of coffee and a warning.

"You won't believe this!"

Lara grabbed the cup. "Thanks. What's wrong, Doris?"

"Those women with the signs yesterday already have a letter about us in this morning's edition of *The Daily Reporter.*"

Making a face, Lara took the paper and sat down, almost spilling her hot coffee. She read aloud the letter in the op-ed section of the paper.

Letter to the Editor

Yesterday a group of concerned, tax-paying citizens confronted the head of our public library to demand the immediate withdrawal of a clearly-inappropriate, licentious book available to any child with a library card. Her response was entirely negative, despite her duty to uphold the highest standards of decency in selecting the materials offered to the public.

According to reports, our Commission intends to award the library a commendation for a recent incident concerning an elderly patron. We demand that such recognition be withheld pending a complete review of library holdings to eliminate the indecent and salacious.

(signed) Mrs. Anna Bozeman, Mrs. Clarabell Friedman, Mrs. Jane Brown, Mrs. Annette Downing, Mrs. Juliette Smith.

"Ouch!" Lara paled, trying to still her trembling coffee hand. "How can we fight this?"

"Charley Moss says we should all attend the next commissioners' meeting and refute these old ninnies. Maybe, show the commissioners our collections."

"And allow their censorship of our holdings? Not on my watch!"

"All right. Then let's get the staff together at closing and get some better ideas."

Lara slapped her forehead. "Maybe I should just resign. That'll satisfy those 'old ninnies,' as you call them."

"Never happen!" Doris swore. "We'll go down together! Fighting!"

Two blocks away, other eyes examined the same letter to the editor over coffee at a local café.

"God," John Schoolfield exclaimed. "Those dames have it in for that Library!"

"Or that efficient, smart Library Director," Dan mused. "We've got to do something to prevent them from harming the Library. Our 4-Hers are now investors in that Library's success. You've got to admit, Lara has been very supportive of our kids and chapters."

John opened his palms. "What can we do?"

"We'll war game this just like old times, John. We did it in Iraq. We can sure outwit some old women in Carrville, Texas."

They sat in silence for several minutes as coffee cups were refilled.

"First," Dan began. "We can write our own letters to the editor, telling everyone how helpful the Library has been to the 4-H and…"

John interrupted the thought. "That's not enough. We need to get that certificate or whatever it is awarded and get the police and fire departments involved, too. They're supposed to get the same recognition as the Library."

"What about those commissioners?"

"We get the Mayor to award all three commendations. We need to get community support, like that slogan about wearing blue on Friday to honor first responders."

Dan suddenly grinned with a thought. "Like 'Wear Blue for the Library, Too?' Great idea, John! You should be mayor!"

"Something to work on, Dan. Let's get started!"

Dan slapped the other's shoulder. "Breakfast is on me! I'll bum paper and pencils from the cashier."

Excitedly, Dan waved at their waitress. "Two plates of good old SOS for my buddy and me!"

"No, you don't," John pulled Dan's hand down. "Steak and eggs, tightwad, for both of us!"

Dan roared. "Afterwards, we'll get to work. I'll do the letters, one from each of us. You work on the ceremony with the Mayor, Police and Fire."

"Where shall we have it?"

"In front of the library, of course!"

"Don't forget the high school band!"

"Plus our 4-Hers, of course."

"And how about our local veterans?"

"Telephone for you, Doris," Amy called from the reference desk.

Standing at the copying machine, Doris nodded. "Thanks, Amy. Just a minute until I get this brute going again. Someone fed it a foreign coin.

"This is Doris Meeker. How may I help you?"

"Hi, Doris, this is Dan Roberts. May I take a moment of your time, without Lara knowing?"

Doris stopped the copier, intrigued that Dan was whispering. "What's up, Dan? Why the secrecy?"

He sighed with relief that Doris didn't hang up. "Lara's irritated at me," he admitted.

Doris already knew that. "Why?"

"She thinks I'm an unscrupulous playboy...or something. Please don't tell her I called you. She won't even talk to me."

"Tell me what you need, Dan."

"I want you to know that John Schoolfield and I are working on a couple of ideas to help the Library. We aim to defuse that poisonous letter to the editor those nasty women sent the newspaper."

Doris exhaled. "Well, thank you. I hope whatever you're planning works. FYI, our staff is meeting after work to brainstorm some ideas, too. Maybe you should tell me what you're planning so we don't conflict."

"Okay, great! I'm writing at least two letters to the editor in defense of the library and John is organizing a ceremony at your place for the Mayor to present those commendations to you, the firemen and police. We hope to have the band there and as many spectators as we can muster.

"But don't tell Lara! If she thinks I'm involved, she'll go ballistic."

Grinning, Doris asked, "Sounds like you're making me your matchmaker. If so, I'm asking that famous question. 'What are your intentions, Mr. Roberts?'"

He gulped before stammering. "Purely honorable! I'd like to be her friend…is all."

Doris enjoyed asking "How good a friend, Mr. Roberts?"

Dan took a deep breath. "Oh, all right, matchmaker! I like her very much! But that's strictly between you and me! Okay?"

Doris smiled as she replaced the receiver.

SEVENTEEN

Eugenia walked into the ladies room the next morning to find Susan there, squinting at the mirror. "What's new, Susan?"

Susan looked up, blinking both eyes. "Damn magnetic eyelashes! Ever try them?"

"Hold on, I think this lash is twisted." Eugenia applied a light touch. "There you go. Better?"

"Yeah, feels okay now. Thanks. You don't wear these things?"

Eugenia was back-combing her graying bangs. "Joe doesn't seem to notice anything about me, unless I'm nude."

Susan paused, an underliner in midair. "Lucky you! I'm still trying to break Art from the bottle and train him with a halter."

Eugenia hiccupped. "What's new with Lara? She looked mad last night at our emergency meeting."

"Worried about what those old women who wrote the newspaper are going to do to us next."

"Between us girls," Eugenia lowered her voice after checking the toilet stalls behind them. "I hear she's in a tizzie about that cowboy who suddenly stopped coming around here."

Susan clapped her hands in glee. "You know what they say about a bachelor?"

Dutifully, Eugnia shook her head.

"He's a guy who never made the same mistake once."

Over at the reference desk, Ceci was signaling Doris she had a phone call. Doris nodded, slowly picking up only after Lara was walking away.

"This is Doris Meeker. May I help you?"

"This is Dan again, Doris. I had another thought about the 'Save Our Library' project. Have you time to hear it?"

Doris stood, straightening her capris. "Tell me."

"I'd like to mail you a draft 'letter to the editor' from Charley's group who come to the library most every day. It's hopefully an example of how much senior citizens depend on your services and periodicals. If it passes the reviews of you and Charley, I'll finalize it and send it to the newspaper with my other letters to the editor. We hope the newspaper will print all of them on the day prior, emphasizing that Friday presentation ceremony we're planning at the Library.

"Make any sense?"

Doris watched Lara close her office door. "Happy to look it over with a caveat. Charley and his buddies have to approve it, too."

"Understood."

"Any other tidbts to share with the ole matchmaker today? Like…you're delivering Lara a dozen red ones tonight when you call?"

Dan snorted. "She won't even talk to me on the phone! She hears my voice and hangs up!"

Doris chuckled. "Don't forget what Napoleon said about persistence."

"What did he say?"

"I forget. Probably something about keep at it.

"Do so, Dan!"

Bruno knocked on his door. Even after he heard Donitz reply 'enter,' Bruno asked "May I come in, sir?"

Donitz beamed. "By all means, Bruno. You are among my most trustworthy colleagues. Too seldom do I express my appreciation for your loyalty during these difficult times for our order."

"I am honored to serve you, sir."

Donitz extended his hand. "What folios have you there?"

Bruno handed him several folios. "Are these for our next meeting at the Carrville library, sir?"

"No, these are for a different purpose entirely. Using the same data from our DNA contact, these folios are of individuals having ancestors who fought *for* our liege, Frederick 1. Astoundingly, they live in the adjacent areas and we'll invite them to our next meeting.

"Why? You are asking." Donitz clapped hands in glee, "These are potential additions to our Hill Country nucleus. They are reinforcements to our dwindling numbers, *not* suspected enemies to be eliminated!"

Bruno was aghast. "As your security officer, sir, how can we possibly be certain of their loyalty to our cause?"

"Excellent question, august Bruno! We must carefully cultivate them like flowers with the doctrine and history of our King and Kaiser, Frederick Barbarossa."

Donitz studied the other man. "We must winnow them like new plants to assure their complete dedication and obedience. It will be add tremendously to your already heavy duties. I'm certain you realize from your extensive security background that our work is now doubly demanding. We must scrutinize these initiates. Some may be seeking entrance into our order for malicious reasons. Like weeds among the petunias, they must be exterminated!"

At this Donitz paused, awaiting a response.

Bruno's answer was immediate. "I understand, sir."

"Then there's that ruffian group who lined the hallway at our last Carrville meeting. Who they are and what they seek is a serious concern. If they appear at our next meeting, they must be dealt with severely."

Bruno answered without further prompting. "Certainly, sir!"

"Sit down, sit down," Donitz gestured to a chair.

Bruno hesitated. He'd never been offered a chair before.

"I thought that perhaps that young man to whom

we left our library complaints about the last Carrville meeting might eventually assist you in your duties. If he forcefully presented our complaints to that female librarian, we should see positive results at our next meeting.

"You remember the man?"

"Yes, sir. His name is Roberts."

Donitz handed the folios back to Bruno. "He bears our scrutiny as well as these potential new additions to our order."

Bruno stood and clicked his heels. "Yes, sir!"

EIGHTEEN

"Steak and eggs?" Dan punched John's shoulder as they took seats at their favorite table in the Norteno restaurant.

"Suppose we flip for our breakfast this time," John winked. "Hate to take your last dime. Your cows may need a new salt lick."

After the steak and eggs had been demolished and coffee cups refilled, they sat back, nodding.

Dan won the coin toss. "Great meal, thanks."

John stretched. "Now we hear status reports, Ole Sarge?"

"You combat medic veterans can get awfully casual once you're discharged and wearin' levis instead of BDU's.

"Nonetheless, I'll start. Okay?

"I've written a draft letter to the editor for the old timers at the library. They are there every day, reading the financial news. Some of them even fall asleep while reading or discussing the Dow, Nasdaq or the S&P 500. The library provides many elderly patrons--and not just this group--a great place to meet, study, meet new people, even learn new skills.

"Those old timers read and approved my draft with a few changes. Their letter to the editor hopefully high-lights the important role the Library plays in supporting people of all ages and interests."

John nodded in approval. "What else are you doing? You're working on another letter, aren't you?"

"I am, Short Round. I'm starting a letter from the two of us, telling how the Library has supported our 4-H clubs with classes, computers, reference materials as well as preparation of individual 4-H projects, and not just those in agriculture."

"They'll be able to compete with college kids once they get there, right?"

Dan looked at his fitbit. "I plan to start writing our letters tonight, once I get home."

John held up a hand. "Thought you were squiring that cute library lady? And instead, you're home with mom and burning the midnight oil?"

"That library director will have nothing to do with me, Stud. She thinks I'm both immoral and lecherous.

"Now to a happier subject, John. How are you doing, organizing that presentation at the library? Still think we can do it by next Friday?"

"Before we move on, Dan, maybe I ought to have a word with the lady in question, to reassure her you ain't entirely immoral and lecherous."

"No, thanks, buddy. Forget it! Her mind is set and no amount of testimonials will change it."

Schoolfield toyed with a spoon. "Then move on to

another pasture. Carla will happily introduce you to several lady friends of hers."

"Back to our subject," Dan demurred. "You were about to brag about your progress in setting up that Friday ceremony with the Mayor."

Exasperated, Schoolfield motioned to the waitress for more coffee. "The Mayor is agreeable as long as I provide him some remarks. The band, majorettes and cheerleaders will parade down the street to the library parking lot. The press will not only be there with a TV van, the newspaper editor has promised me a color header on the Thursday and Friday front pages reading 'Wear Blue for the Library, Too!'"

"Sounds like a great start, John. Thanks. How may I help you?

"Make me happy by calling that Library Director and inviting her outside next Friday for our ceremony. Flowers might be appropriate, don't you think?"

Dan growled. "Forget her! Let's concentrate on that Friday ceremony!"

Later that day, Doris called Lara in her office "There's that 4-H man here to see you, Lara. Shall I send him down this way?"

Lara gasped, thinking Doris meant Dan. Recovering, she asked, "Which 4-H man?"

"Not the cowboy, the other one. John Schoolfield."

"Does he look dangerous?"

"Not at all."

"Then send him back."

Lara met John at her open door. "How may I help you, Mr. Schoolfield?"

He removed an army embroidered baseball cap. "Call me John, please. May I see you a minute? I need serious talk with you about…"

A scream of pain from the third floor interrupted her reply. Instead, she dropped her appointment book. "God! What's that?"

"Sounds like intense pain! Somebody's hurting big time!" John turned and began double-timing down the hall.

"I'm right behind you!" Lara followed, trying to keep up. "Let's use the elevator," she screeched, but he was already running up the stairs to the third floor.

There they saw a young woman on her knees outside the Conference Room, her skirt soaked and a pool of liquid around her.

"Help me! My water broke!"

"Call 911!" John commanded. "Quick! She's having a baby!"

By then Doris and Amy had joined them. Doris whipped out her cellphone and dialed 911 for assistance.

"Amy, keep everyone out!" Lara yelled, helping the woman to her feet.

"In here," John took the woman's other arm and led her into the Conference Room. He easily lifted her onto the table.

Lara's voice waivered as she watched John remove his jacket and roll it up. "For her head," John mumbled, feeling the woman's arm for a pulse.

"I think the baby's coming soon, real soon." He looked at Doris. "Get me some sharp scissors and a big paper clasp."

A wide-eyed Lara demanded, "Do you know what you're doing? Shouldn't we rush her to the hospital?"

On the table the woman was screaming and crying as John tried instructions and reassurance. "Take deep breaths! You're doing fine! Everything's all right!"

"Do you know what you're doing?" Lara repeated, punching John on the shoulder as hard as she could.

"Stop hitting me. I was a medic and delivered several babies in Iraq. I can do it here, too."

He grinned. "As Dan would say, this ain't my first rodeo."

At the name, Lara bit her lip.

"Quick, get me as many towels as you can," he told Doris as she handed him scissors and a paper clasp. "Maybe a blanket, too?"

"Cut her panties away and get 'em off. Find something clean on which we can deliver this baby.

"Where's that ambulance?" John yelled.

"On the way," Amy replied from the door where she stood guard.

"Tell them where we're at!"

"Will do."

Amid the cacophony of moans and cries, John asked Lara to hold the woman's hand and try to comfort her. "Remind her 'Rapid and shallow breathing' during the contractions."

Shaken, Lara asked, "Will the baby come soon?"

John's forehead sparkled with sweat. "Yes, I think so. I bet our baby beats the ambulance here."

Doris chortled. "Another first for our Library!

"What name should we give it?"

Continuing the charade, Doris said, "The babe's being born nearest the Texana stacks. We'll call her 'Texana.'"

"What if it's a boy?"

"Hush, you two!" John spoke sharply. "I've got to concentrate and remember what to do."

Suddenly, his voice deepened as he directed the soon-to-be mother. "Push! Push now! Keep it up!"

"Push. Push. Push."

The baby's head slowly began emerging. John carefully extracted the infant and cradled it in his arms. He cut the umbilical cord with the scissors and applied the paper clasp to stop bleeding.

John wacked the baby's bottom and the newborn immediately wailed. "Hear that?" he chortled. "She's telling us she's fine and happy to be here!"

Amy clamped her hands over her mouth. "Look at all that blood! What's that white ooze? Is she okay?"

John laughed. That's the gift wrapping babies arrive in, called vermix."

"A girl?" Doris repeated. "And born in our Library!"

At the sound of the baby's cries, the new mother opened her eyes and John nestled the tiny baby in her arms.

As the ambulance attendants rushed in, taking

charge, Lara sat down heavily in one of the conference chairs. She grinned. "We'll need another commemorative plaque!"

She turned her attention to John, flopping in another chair and studying his bloody hands.

"Congratulations, John! Great job! By the way, what was it you wanted to talk to me about downstairs?"

NINETEEN

Dan was already at their usual restaurant table the next morning. He brandished the morning paper at John, entering the front door.

Instead of a 'good morning,' an angry Dan flattened his fist on the table. "What the hell were you doin' behind my back at the Library yesterday?"

Unperturbed, John motioned for the waitress, studied the menu (which he knew by heart) and ordered breakfast.

Turning to his friend, he asked. "What were you saying, Ole Sarge?"

"See this?" Dan pointed to a photograph on the front page. The caption read,

"LIBRARY WELCOMES NEWEST PATRON"

Lara, John, Doris and Amy appeared in the photograph surrounding a tiny new infant held by her jubilant mother.

"Well, yeah," John admitted. "I was there for a bit, checking on equipment for the Friday ceremony.

You know, chairs, podium, flags, sound system, stuff like that."

Dan interrupted. "You look mighty cozy with the Library Director here," he pointed.

"Okay, Dan. Be cool! Not only was I that baby's deliverer, I also had a chance to plead your case with Lara. She seemed very interested in what I told her."

"You promised to keep out of it!"

"I don't recall those words."

"Well, what did you tell her?"

"Say 'Please,' first."

"Please, hell! Tell me or you're leaving here in a body bag."

John sipped his coffee "That ain't funny, Dan."

He took another sip."

"I told her you were a chum, never known to lie or even pull girls' pigtails. In short, I built you up higher than the Washington Monument. I even told her your efforts of late on her library's behalf."

Since Dan was silent, John added, "You're welcome. And 'yes' you may buy our breakfast in light of my myriad efforts on your behalf yesterday."

Later, Dan stood up, check in hand. John stammered, "Wait, Dan. Where are you off to in such a hurry?"

"I'm first out the gate. Got plenty of work to do at home which I've been neglecting. See you here in the morning!"

The next morning, it was John's turn to be 'first out the gate.' Armed with the morning newspaper, he sat down for coffee. As Dan entered the front door, John glowered at him.

"Your turn, Ole Sarge! Tell me why I didn't get to see these letters before you sent them to the newspaper!"

He pointed at the op-ed page.

LETTER TO THE EDITOR

Dear Editor: We, the undersigned, want to acknowledge the superior support offered our respective 4-H Clubs of Carr and Kandall Counties by the Director and Staff of the Carrville Public Library.

At our request, the Library designed a special program for our youths to not only acquaint them with the extensive facilities of the Library, but to train them in their use. Thus equipped, our 4-Hers will be prepared to compete with older students at the university level.

The training program designed and executed by library personnel included citizenship, money management, conservation of natural resources, nutrition, physical health, safety and mathematics. As you see, the programs presented our youngsters by the Library were both ambitious and extensive.

It was eagerly received by over 100 4-H youths, each of whom now is not only a regular, official patron, but an enthusiastic advocate of the Carrville Public Library.

We think your readers should know of their Library's excellence.

Show your support by attending the Mayor's commendatory award ceremony at the Library, Friday at 10:00 a.m.

We wear blue for our first responders to show our pride in them, let's wear blue on Friday to accord our great Library that same recognition!

See you there!

Sincerely, John Schoolfield and Dan Roberts, Advisors of the Carr and Kandall Counties 4-H Clubs.

"Not a bad write-up, Dan. Why didn't you share it with me first?"

Roberts grinned. "You mean like you shared with me that you'd gone behind my back the other day at the Library?"

Chagrinned, John switched his attention to the next letter.

TO THE EDITOR:

None of us (our names are signed at the bottom) have written you a letter before. We think it time to bring to your (and the public's) attention what a great service the public library provides us elderly patrons. Not only can we go there to read the latest periodicals (particularly about stock market shenanigans) but also share experiences and knowledge with others.

For example, one of us conducts the 'Storyteller' reading session for ages 4-6 in the Library every Wednesday morning. The Library offers lots of opportunities for all ages, not just us oldies.

What we're trying to say (excuse any grammer or spelling mistakes) is that the Library is a humdinger and deserves everyone's praise and support.

Respectfully submitted (but we'd sure like to see our letter in your fine newspaper.)

(signed) Charles Moss, Roscoe Waller, Anson Brown, Pete Tejada, Amos Philpott

"How'd you like that one?" Dan signaled the waitress for more coffee.

"I'm almost crying," John joked. "No, it's good, Dan. Real good. You could be a speech writer for the President.

"Speaking of that, here are my draft comments for Mr. Mayor to use at our ceremony Friday. How about casting your literary eye on them?"

John pointed to the two letters to the editor. "Unlike your products, which I never saw before they were published today."

"Okay, Short Round. I apologize and will be happy to look at your comments for the Mayor. What about a program for the ceremony?"

"Already in the works, Dan. Not to worry."

TWENTY

D oris rapped on Lara's door. "That 4-H man is out front again and asking to see you."

Anticipating Lara's question, Doris added, "No, *not* Dan."

"Okay. Send him back. How about sitting in with us, just to make sure he doesn't open the door with an 'Oops! Here's Dan!'"

Once seated at Lara's small conference table, John Schoolfield passed out papers. "Thanks for seeing me, Lara."

"John," she acknowledged.

"I'm here to discuss with you ladies the program for the awards ceremony since it's going to beheld here Friday in front of your Library."

"Pray for sunshine," Doris offered.

"Good point," Lara frowned, "since we don't have sufficient space inside the library for a backup venue."

"How about in the front area, where the books are checked out?"

Lara shook her head. "Too small. How big a crowd do you expect?"

"At least a hundred," John tapped a pencil against his teeth.

"Then we'll just have to postpone and reschedule the ceremony if we're rained out."

John nodded and made a note. "Using our 4-Hers, we'll place your podium on the top step and four chairs behind it," he pointed to a diagram on the paper.

"Who sits where?" Doris asked.

"The Mayor and the three recipients, Fire, Police and you," he nodded at Lara.

"The first row of chairs in the audience is reserved for the commissioners.

"The band marches down the street, turns in here," he continued, pointing, "and sits there."

"Have you enough chairs lined-up?" Lara asked.

"We can seat one hundred folks. More than that will have to stand but we plan for the ceremony to be short and sweet. Even the Mayor agreed to be quick!"

Lara smiled. "Nice work, John."

"So we start with the National Anthem, played by the band, then everybody sits down.

"Oh...I didn't mention the honor guard precedes the band, presents the colors in front of the podium, then retires after the National Anthem."

"What about a prayer?" Doris leaned forward.

John tapped his teeth again. "Yeah, a prayer follows the National Anthem and the colors marching away."

Lara made a note on her paper, looking up. "Who is it?"

"We have someone picked out and prepared."

She repeated. "Who?

"A minister," John blinked.

"Who, John?"

"His name is…Dan Roberts."

Irritated with the answer, Lara stared at him. "Not funny, John! Is this your idea of a joke?"

"No, it's not a joke, Lara. I think you've misjudged Dan. He's a lay minister. I guarantee he'll deliver a memorable prayer. Let's finish this draft and go back to the prayer later, if you insist."

Ignoring Lara's angry brow, John continued. "Next, I introduce the Mayor and he makes a few remarks and presents the three certificates to the Police Chief, Fire Chief and Library Director." He rolled his eyes at Lara, still irate.

"Meanwhile, the TV crew and news reporters are doing their thing.

"That's it! The ceremony is over and everybody breaks for lunch or whatever."

Hopefully, John addressed Doris. "What do you think?"

"It's up to Lara, not me," she motioned.

Suddenly, Lara was on her feet and out the door.

John picked up his papers. "I hope that was an affirmative answer."

Understanding her friend's reaction, Doris sighed. "She's bewildered. Tell Dan to call her again and take her out some place tonight."

She opened her apartment door after studying him through the peep hole.

He stood there, awkwardly holding another bouquet of flowers.

"You're a brave man," she began, "coming here without so much as a phone call."

He shook his head. "You wouldn't have answered or would have yelled 'Don't come!'"

Like an attorney, she quickly followed up. "You didn't tell me you were a minister. Why?"

"You wouldn't have believed me. Besides," he handed her the flowers, "I'm not a regular. Just do it to help out my little farming community."

"Since you're here," she smiled, "and I've accepted your flowers, you might as well come in and have a beer."

Relieved, Dan entered. "I was hoping you'd say that."

He opened the refrigerator. "Since I know where the beer's at, may I do the honors?"

"You may, Mr. Roberts of constant surprises. Wait! Ministers don't drink beer!"

"This one does," he handed her an opened bottle.

They clicked bottles. "Cheers!"

"How about some popcorn?"

"Can't, Miss Beyer. Popcorn might spoil your appetite. I'm taking you out to dine."

Amused by his mood, she said, "Oh?"

"Doris told John and John told me to take you out

tonight. Nothing fancy," he saw her hesitation. "Just you, me and pizza."

"I'll overlook the grammar," she teased. "Will Doris and John be there, too?"

"Nope. I want you all to myself for some serious talk.

"But, first, PIZZA!"

Later, at Lara's apartment, he left. After turning and twisting on her rumpled bed, she gave up. "Sleep eludes me," she admitted to the pillow. Surrendering, she retreated to the sofa and turned on the CD player.

She gasped, as the lyrics began.

> *"I've gotta whole lot of kissin'*
> *For you!,*
> *I've gotta whole lot of lovin'*
> *For you!"*

Blocks away in the exclusive Summit neighborhood of town, a different meeting was taking place.

Anna Bozeman greeted each arriving lady at her ranch-style home with a baby orchid and glass of champagne. Once all the guests had arrived, she treated them to more champagne and an array of finger food delicacies in a massive dining room.

She stood and raised her glass to begin the meeting. "Thank you all for coming to this, our final, checklist meeting. By all accounts, our previous planning sessions were so productive that this meeting may be a short one.

"To reiterate, our objective is to prevent...or at least disrupt...what our husbands were unable to accomplish. Of course I mean the achievement award for that smut-filled library, which we all support with our hard earned work and taxes.

"Shouldn't our voices be heard when the library's not run decently?

"Well, we found a chief librarian, or whatever her title, oblivious to the need to eliminate all objectionable, salacious literature from our library. Hence, we will take action, as would any clear-minded citizen, to achieve our objective.

"DRAIN THE LIBRARY OF SMUT!"

"I turn now to the ingenious lady having responsibility for accomplishing previously discussed Plan A, limiting foot and vehicular access to the library tomorrow. Clarabell, have you gathered sufficient drivers and vehicles to do the job?"

In a loud voice, Clarabell answered proudly. "Yes, I have! We are ready to rumble!"

Her enthusiasm caused a ripple of applause from the others.

"Thank you for your detailed planning which will result in temporary paralysis of traffic around the library! Well done!"

Anna led the others in sustained applause.

"Now we turn our attention to Plan B, the responsibility of Jane and her ladies. Have we enough signs and posters for tomorrow's demonstration?"

Not to be out done, Jane rose from her chair. "We have plenty of attention-getting signs and enthusiastic sign carriers. We will make a tremendous impression on any public remaining after Plan A's implementation!"

"Excellent!" Another round of applause followed.

As the applause diminished, a hand was raised. "Question, please."

"Yes, Juliette?"

"Have we considered that some of our members," her wave extended to everyone, "may be arrested by the police?"

"We considered that briefly," Anna conceded, smiling. "But what Carrville policeman would dare ticket--much less arrest--the wife of a Carrville commissioner?"

Laughter followed, sparked by more bubbly.

TWENTY ONE

"Hey, John, what's the problem up there? We're not moving at all. Traffic's deadlocked here on Earl Garrett Street!"

Dan held his phone closer to hear over the clamor of honking horns. The van, packed with fifty members of his 4-H chapter, was sandwiched between yellow school buses carrying the band to Water Street where it would begin marching to the Library.

"No one's moving up here, either, Dan. I can see three SUVs blocking the street to the Library. We should have started an hour earlier. My kids are getting antsy just sitting here. Unless those big SUVs are towed away soon, we won't make it to the Library by 10:00 unless we hoof it."

Dan looked over his shoulder at his own 4-Hers who, too, looked rattled by the din and traffic "Maybe that's our best option, John."

John's tone changed. "There's a policeman up there. I'll hop off the van and see what he says. What a mess!"

"Let me know, please." Dan looked behind his van. "Cars and trucks are backed up all the way to the courthouse. This turmoil had to be planned, to delay the library ceremony. Who could have done it?"

John returned from talking to the policeman. "Cops want to bring in wreckers to tow those three SUVs blocking traffic, but the wreckers can't get through, either. They don't know yet the owners of those three SUVs. They ought to be prosecuted!

"As to your question, who hates the Library this much to sabotage our ceremony? I'm reminded of those women carrying signs at the Library the other day."

"Yeah," Dan agreed. "That's the same ones who sent that letter to the editor, complaining about the Library.

"See you there, John! We're getting off our van and walking."

"What about the van?"

"I'm leaving the driver to take care of it. Eventually, we'll see our vans after the ceremony. Looks like the band is getting out of their buses, too, and carrying their instruments toward the Library."

Twenty minutes later, the 4-Hers, majorettes, cheerleaders and band, and lots of spectators, had reached the Library and seated themselves in front of the podium.

Covering the front of the Library was a huge 4-H-made sign reading

'WEAR BLUE FOR THE LIBRARY, TOO!'

Minutes later, the commissioners arrived, took their seats on the front row and began shaking hands with everyone available.

Lara stood at the podium, wearing a pale blue dress and stiletto heels. "Where've you been?" she demanded, checking her watch.

"You look like a million dollars," Dan exhaled. "Sorry I'm late! Everybody's late due to some SUVs blocking the street. Traffic is snarled all the way downtown.

"We," his hand indicated the band already taking seats and tuning up, "had to walk the last several blocks to get here. We'll have to be flexible with the timing of this ceremony."

Dan repressed an urge to kiss her despite the gawking crowd, mostly dressed in shades of blue. Instead, he grinned at her. "You look marvelous."

John rushed up, pointing. "Here come the Fire Chief and the Police Chief. They look furious." He indicated to them their positions beside Lara.

"I see the Mayor is almost here as well," Dan observed. "Late or not, let's get this show on the road."

John looked heavenward. "At least we have sunshine! The sound system is on and the band looks ready to play at my signal."

Dan volunteered. "I'll go help the Mayor up the steps to the podium. Once he's in place we can ..."

Suddenly, angry female voices rang out from behind the seated 4-Hers, band and spectators. A dozen women, wavlng hand-made signs and posters, began shouting in front.

"What now?" Lara paled, staring at the signs and angry faces.

DRAIN THE LIBRARY!

RID THE LIBRARY OF FILTHY BOOKS!

BURN BAD BOOKS!

Several placards being waved at Lara caused Dan to step in front of her.

IF YOU DON'T ACT, WE WILL!

BAN 50 SHADES AND CLONES!

The audience, including the Mayor, seemed mesmerized by the signs and chants from the elderly ladies. Seeing several of their wives in the demonstration, some commissioners paled and tried to hide. The Police Chief grabbed his phone, ordering police assistance.

Dan tugged at John's blue shirt sleeve. "Signal the band to play the National Anthem! That should stop those crazies!"

John signaled the band leader to play and the musicians responded immediately. The effect was as sudden as the shock of the demonstration.

At the sounds of the National Anthem, everyone

stood and began singing along with Lara. Keeping time with her hands, she urged everyone to join her. And they did!

Even the demonstrating females stopped chanting and, embarrassed, joined the singing. Several dropped their placards or hid their faces as cameras began flashing.

Clearing his throat, the Mayor straightened his tie and began a short speech of welcome and congratulations to the Police Chief, Fire Chief and Library Director for their excellent service to the community. The Mayor presented framed awards to each of the three, amid applause from the spectators and more photos by reporters and the recently arrived TV crew.

At another signal, the band began playing a medley as the crowd broke up and headed downtown. After thanking the Mayor for his participation, amid more photos and handshakes, John grabbed Dan's arm.

"Sorry, we had to skip your prayer, Dan. That demonstration screwed up our timing."

Lara proudly held her award aloft as Dan hugged her. The prayer was forgotten.

By the time the band finished its musical medley, traffic on Water Street was partially cleared. Wreckers arrived to tow away the three big SUVs which had blocked the street. Several of the commissioners grimly watched their wives' vehicles being ticketed and towed.

Soon the only residue of the brief ceremony was a

pile of discarded signs which the women flaunted as the ceremony began. Clarice gathered them up and began taking them inside.

Lara and Dan helped her carry them through the back door. "I think we ought to keep these, have another party and burn 'em. Maybe get photos of all our gals holding the Mayor's certificate?"

Lara and Dan whooped agreement.

TWENTY TWO

"**N**O!" the man sitting at the keyboard exclaimed loudly enough to be heard throughout the Library's first floor. The speaker, Roscoe Waller, was easily the most taciturn member of the elderly group who claimed the financial periodicals each morning.

"What's wrong, Roscoe?" An alarmed Anson Brown patted his friend on the shoulder. "Did the computer reject your password again?"

"Agh! Wish it were that easy! This darned website says I'm overdue on my fees and will cut me off unless I pay up immediately. I owe a hundred dollars to the hungry beast."

"What website is that?"

Roscoe rolled his eyes, not wanting to reveal its name or nature. "Just a harmless little club I joined."

This time Anson pounded the other's back in glee. "Bet it's one of them porno places. Don't worry, Roscoe, I won't tell the others.

"Which one is it? Does it cost a lot? Is it worth the money?"

"Just a slight technical problem," Roscoe lied. "Maybe one of the librarians can help me solve it."

Looking around the room, he spotted Amy Sidwell, who had taught him how to use a password to enter the internet.

Uncomfortable, he sat and glared at the offending terminal. "What a fix! Can't afford another month with *Route60.com.* and I was just getting the hang of it.

"Who can help me? If I ask one of my buddies, the word will get around to everyone of 'em. They'd all laugh their asses off and make fun of me. If I ask a woman, I'd be mighty embarrassed to explain my problem."

Frustrated, he stalked out the front door and sat down on the library steps. Clarice, the housekeeper barely known to him, came out and began sweeping the steps.

He worked up his courage to speak. "Good morning, Miss Clarice. Nice day, ain't it?"

"Well, Roscoe," she stopped and eyed him as he began to stand. "What a surprise! Didn't think you even knew my name!"

"Everybody knows you, Ma'm. Hard worker. Nice lady."

"Well, thank you, Roscoe. With that buildup, there must be something I can do for you?"

By now, Roscoe was breathing hard, like a cross-country runner. He managed another "Yes, ma'm.

"There is a mighty big favor…a confidential one… I'd like to ask of you. If you don't mind, that is," he quickly added, hoping she'd refuse.

She appraised him silently before deciding. "Well,

if it's something confidential, we can't talk about it out here. Come to the kitchen in a few minutes. It's mostly deserted this time of day. You can ask me that confidential favor there. Okay?"

Roscoe felt like throwing his baseball cap into the air and whooping. He toned it down to a "Bless you, Miss Clarice. I'll be there in a shake."

As she predicted, the kitchen was deserted. They helped themselves to coffee and sat down opposite each other at the long table.

"Well, Roscoe, what's on your mind?"

He gulped, thinking he'd blundered too far but couldn't back out now. "Strictly confidential, right, Miss Clarice?"

"Quit calling me 'Miss,' Roscoe. Spit it out, whatever's bothering you. Maybe I can help, maybe not."

"But confidential, right?"

"Yes, Roscoe! Confidential! Go ahead."

He closed his eyes momentarily, steeling himself for what he must admit.

"I secretly joined a get-acquainted site on one of the Library's computers."

Clarice tried not to smile, even grin, at this revelation. "Go ahead," she managed with a straight face.

His eyes implored understanding "It costs money, a monthly fee, to meet ladies on that darned internet. You won't understand, but gents...even like me...need occasional companionship. The good ole boys just ain't enough.

"But the ladies I saw on *Route 60: A Discreet Dating Site For 60-Plus* are older, some even uglier than me!"

She injected smoothly, "Why, you're a fine looking man, Roscoe."

He stared at her, dumbfounded. "Huh?"

"You heard me. You haven't told me your problem yet. Spit it out."

He looked down at his hands. "I can't afford *Route 60* no more. And I didn't meet anyone there I'd want to take out. What should I do?"

"What's your password to that site?"

Roscoe lowered his head but whispered the answer. "Sweetie Pie."

Instead of grinning, she turned authoritative. "Forget that silly dating site, Roscoe! Never use that password again! Save your money! You'll meet a nice lady right here in Carrville, I'll bet."

He stared at her, then exhaled, more confident than he had felt in years.

"Would you go out with me, Clarice?"

TWENTY THREE

Coffee was brewing in the staff lounge, presided over by Clarice. Lara was the first through the door, looking for her personal coffee cup amid the usual clutter of china.

"Good morning Clarice," she poured herself a cup, eyeing Clarice again.

"You look radiant this morning, Clarice. Is it vitamins, a blush blend or a new boy friend?"

Clarice's grin widened. "You're sharp as a new knife, Boss. Roscoe--you remember him from our famous Financial News Nodders?--took me out to eat last night."

Lara sighed, remembering her own dinner with Dan. "I hope you had a great time?"

Clarice sighed. "It may be too early, but I think I've found a keeper."

Amy, wearing a new lace blouse, paraded proudly before them. Hearing Clarice, Amy exclaimed "Good luck with that! I'm ready to return Harold for a refund! I may put an ad in the paper. Anybody interested?"

Clarice and Lara shook their heads in unison.

Amy made a face as she sipped the hot coffee. "What's the *good* news, if any?"

"According to the newspapers and TV, our Friday ceremony was a huge success," Lara announced. "On the other side of the coin, that strange historical group will be using our conference room this week. The last time they were here, they complained about some of the 'Nodders' making faces and gestures at them.

"Oddly enough, Dan Roberts relayed their complaint to me. I still haven't figured that out," her forehead wrinkled, "but I will!"

Charley Moss shuffled his feet beside the reference desk, waiting for the *Wall Street Journal* to be handed him by Doris. "Thank you kindly, Miss Doris."

She looked up at him quizzically. "I need a word with you, as soon as you're available, for a little private chat about what's happening this week."

"Yes, Ma'm. Charley's always available."

"See you in there," she pointed at the Young Adult reading room, "as soon as you're finished memorizing that *Journal*."

Half an hour later, she joined Charley in the reading room.

Frowning, he touched his beard. "Am I in trouble agin?"

"No, Charley, not yet. But you *will* be in deep doo-doo if you don't listen to what I'm about to tell you."

"Got my ears on!" Charley responded dutifully.

She paused, remembering his recent memory

lapses. "Remember that strange group here last month that used our Conference Room?"

"Of course I do!" Charley made a face. "Didn't like them! There was something downright suspicious about them and what they claimed they wuz studying."

"They're coming back Tuesday and we've got to respect their being here," she slapped the table, "just like we do everybody else, including your buddies.

"That Conference Room is not the private domain of you and your friends. This is a public library. Do you read me, Charley?

"Last time they complained about the antics of your bunch."

Charley sat straighter in his chair. Indignant, he asked, "What did they say?"

Having talked with Lara earlier that day, Doris remembered the complaints. "They said you banged on the Conference Room door and tried to get in to disrupt their meeting."

He folded his arms on his chest. "We was just checkin' to make sure that door could be opened in case of fire."

"They also complained that you guys stood in the hallway and made faces and nasty remarks about them as they departed."

"Well, that hallway belongs to everyone, don't it?"

She smacked the desk again. "Stop that right now! Leave them alone! If they complain again about rudeness or misconduct, we might cancel all your library cards! You won't be able to use, even come here any more!"

Charley rubbed his chin. "Thought we wuz friends, Miss Doris."

"We are, if y'all obey the rules. If not, you'll be kicked out of this Library! Clear?"

Silently, he arose and walked slowly out the room, then out of the library.

She watched his slow progress, sighed and returned to her reference desk. "Damn! If they were gone, I'd sure miss those old 'Snorers.'"

The next morning Charley presided at the coffee klasch of the "Financial News Nodders" held in the Norteno restaurant where they received free seconds. He rattled a spoon against his cup.

Anson Brown interrupted a slurp of hot coffee. "What's up, Charley?"

Charley scowled to assure their attention. "Secret business is what.

"Everybody remember that peculiar group of strangers we escorted out of the Conference Room not long ago?"

Everyone nodded attentively, even setting down their cups.

"Well, they're coming back to our Library and have reserved our fine Conference Room again. This time we gotta' find out what they're up to, which I think is no good.

"They might be terrorists for all we know! So our

first job--like a military objective—is to find out what they're doing and prevent it, if it's something bad."

Roscoe Waller snickered. "Why don't we just invite them here to join us for coffee and ask them 'What's your business?'"

"That ain't funny, Roscoe! Those people may pose a real threat to the Library. Maybe they plan on blowing it to smithereens...or something."

"What are you proposing, Charley Moss?"

Another voice resounded. "More coffee, please," to the waitress, then to Charley. "Don't be getting' us in trouble again with that nice Library Director. We need the Library, that's our home-away-from-home."

Angrily, Charley retorted. "That's why we must find out what these strangers are up to! If we don't take action, we might not have a Library any more!"

"Okay, okay, Charley," Roscoe raised his hand. "What's your plan to accomplish this military objective, as you call it?"

Charley leaned back in his chair. "First, I want everyone's agreement that what I'm about to say is secret, just like those Pentagon papers! None of us can tell anyone outside this table what we're talkin' about. Agreed?"

"You've been seeing too many 'Don't Watch Alone' scare shows on TV!"

Charley eyed his critic. "If you can't agree to keep our business secret, John, get outa' here right now!"

Nobody stirred.

Taking a sheaf of paper from his overalls, Charley

donned bifocals and looked over his solemn captives. "If you have questions, I'd appreciate you holding them 'til I'm done with my notes here.

"First, we need to find out why these strangers want to meet in our Library. They reserved the Conference Room again, so we need to know what they talk about in there. To do this, we need to put a microphone behind that big TV screen in there.

"Luckily, we have an expert, retired from the phone company. Amos will install a small microphone which we can listen to in the room next door. We need several volunteers to sit in that room and take notes about what is said."

"Why not record it, instead?"

Despite his plea to ask questions later, Charley nodded, looking at Amos. "Can we do that?"

"Sure. Can do. But why do we need a recording?"

"In case we want to submit our evidence to the FBI. Tom, here, is a retired agent, He'll know who we should contact."

Tom spoke up. "If we have real evidence of criminal activity, we need to identify each member of this group. Photographs are essential."

Anxious to contribute, Roscoe raised a hand "I've a great little reflex camera. Maybe I could get a shot of each individual as he enters the Library Tuesday."

"Or departs," Anson added.

"When are they supposed to arrive?"

"They reserved the Conference Room as before, from ten until one."

"Are they from out-of-town?"

Charley shook his head. "Anyone know?"

"We could check the hotels and motels. If we knew where they stayed the last time, they'll probably roost there again," Phil offered.

"Can you check around for that Phil?"

"Consider it done."

The waitress presented a bill for their coffee which Charley grabbed. "Thanks to y'all, this has been a useful pow-wow and I'm getting the check. My treat!"

On the way out, someone asked, "Shouldn't we meet again, to make sure everything's ready?"

"Same time, here, tomorrow," Charley called out. "But I can't guarantee I'll pick up this durned check again!"

TWENTY FOUR

"Is this another of your tricks, Cowboy?"

"Yes, Ma'm," he admitted. "But it's not the kind of trick you accused me of earlier."

They were entering the Mountan Inn dining room and he led her to a table in the rear. A smiling, elderly woman rose to meet them.

"Mom, this is Lara, of whom I've often spoken."

Lara looked shocked. "Pleased to meet you, Mrs. Roberts. Your tricky son is a constant surprise."

"You!" Frustrated by this surprise, she punched his shoulder.

"This ain't my first rodeo, Lara," he laughed. "I had to scheme a bit to get the two of you together."

Dan's mother chuckled. "He can be a sneak, can't he?

"Seems like I know you already, Lara. Dan talks about you all the time. I'm tickled that we finally get to meet each other."

Dinner eventually over, the two ladies still compared notes and stories. His mother showed Lara old photos of Dan on his first pony, Dan at Boy Scout summer camp, Dan during his deployment to Iraq, amid dozens of others.

"That's enough, Mom! You're boring Lara to death! Let her finish her dessert!"

"This is better than banana cream pie!" Lara exclaimed. "I've gathered enough tease data on you tonight that I can use for years."

Mrs. Roberts cackled. "Sounds like this lovely lady may have long term plans for you, Son!"

"I'm lucky, Mom," he admitted. Pointing at his mother, "You are my witness to what she said!"

He grabbed Lara's hand, "And I'm just liable to hold you to a long term commitment."

Mrs. Roberts arose from the table. "Time for me to skedaddle. You two need to talk without this old woman. Please come to see me, Lara. Any time."

With that, she walked out.

Lara looked alarmed. "Will she be all right? Can she get home okay?"

"Sure. She's fiercely independent, just like you."

The two of them talked until past closing time. Finally, he drove her home where they began a deeper conversation yet.

"Amos, is that microphone working? Charley stood looking into the Conference Room.

"Like a charm, like a charm!" Proudly, Amos saluted his workmanship. "See, I installed it in the back of this TV. All you can see is this tiny little black wire going into this junction box," he pointed.

"Then the wire goes to a small speaker in the next room where we record their conversation or take notes."

"Nice job, Amos. What about your camera?" Charley turned to Roscoe who joined them in the hallway.

"Probably best if I can get individual pictures, without their noticing, as they leave the room here. The hall's narrow enough, they'll have to come out one at a time."

"What if they see you and hide their faces?"

"I'll be in this supply closet and snap their photos through a crack in the door."

"Do your best to get a good likeness of each one."

"Will do, Charley."

Later at the group's meeting in the restaurant, Phil gave his lodgings report. "Last month, they all stayed at the Mountain Inn. If they go there again, I should be able to get a copy of their registrations from the night clerk, my cousin on Mother's side."

"Thanks, sounds good, Phil. Any questions?"

A hand was raised by Joe Cotton. "I got a suggestion, not a question. If we want to get rid of these characters, why don't we serve 'em free coffee in the Conference Room?"

Everyone was puzzled. "Free coffee?"

"Sure. Free coffee laced with a little laxative to make them immediately bolt to the mens' room."

"That would be a pretty sight," someone laughed.

"Let's do it!"

In the staff coffee lounge, Amy held everyone's attention. "She had a highlight put in her hair. Looks mighty glamorous!"

"Lara sure looks serious at that Dan fellow."

"He can't keep his eyes off her when he's in the Library," observed Susan, flipping back her lounge hoodie.

Doris held up the hand to which she'd been applying nail polish. "I've got bigger news than that!" she said smugly. "Once you hear it, you all may want to revise our bets about when their engagement will be announced."

"Oh, no!" Clarice was the first to object. "We all agreed there could be no changes!"

Eugenia sniffed at her. "You'd love to change your bet, wouldn't you? You said you wrote in 'Never happen,' that they'd never get married."

"What's your big news, Doris?"

Grinning broadly, Doris looked up from her nails. "Hold on to your hats! Last night she met Dan's mother!"

The lounge reverberated with "Ohhhs!"

"Then I want to update my guess, too!" Ceci cried.

A chorus of 'Me, too's ended the coffee break as they returned to work.

"Is this Mr. Dan Roberts?"

All morning, Dan had been cutting and putting up oats to feed his cattle. When he came in at noon for soup and sandwich, his mother told him about the telephone call.

"A Mr. Don-its, or something like that," she said. "He left an 800 number for you to call."

At his frown, she asked, "Something wrong, Dan?"

"He's a strange bird, Mom, probably wants something from me. Last time he asked me to tell Lara the complaints about his visit to the Library, instead of telling her directly.

"Well, I did it, out of courtesy. Now she thinks I'm in cahoots with this guy and his group."

"Who are they?"

He dialed the 800 number before answering. "I hear they study medieval history about Germany and some old king. Were I to help Donitz again, she'd get mad at me all over."

"Then tell him 'no,' Son. Sounds simple to me," she poured him a glass of milk.

"Yes, this is Dan Roberts."

"Good morning, sir." Donitz's voice echoed in the old-fashioned kitchen after Dan turned on the speaker phone. "Thank you for your previous assistance at the library. I have another proposal which you might find interesting as well as profitable,"

Dan sighed and sat down at the kitchen table, thinking 'I might as well hear him out if it could benefit Lara.'

"What kind of proposal?"

"It's of a sensitive nature, better explained in

person. Can we meet somewhere in Carrville at your convenience?"

"Ten o'clock tomorrow morning at the Norteno restaurant?"

"Fine, thank you. I'm sure you will find my proposal most intriguing. Goodbye."

He sat for a moment before drinking the milk. "What do you think, Mom?"

"I don't understand why you agreed since you apparently dislike the feller."

He held up his hands. "Maybe it's something that I can help Lara with."

She said, rather than asked, "You really like her, don't you?"

A wide grin was her answer

She nodded understanding. "Well, good luck, but be smart as a rattlesnake with that Don-its."

Although they had not reserved the Conference Room, that's where Charley wanted to hold the next meeting of the 'Nodders.'

"We need to double check every plan," he explained, "because our suspects will be here tomorrow."

"Tell me again what they're suspected of, Charley?" Anson asked.

Charley rubbed his forehead. "We don't know specifically, Anson, until they get in this very room and reveal their plans.

"They may want to poison our water supply, release anthrax at the hospital... who knows? That's why we've got to be prepared before they sit in these very seats we're in right now."

"Somebody's got to take up the slack, Anson." Joe Cotton stood up. "Who better than us?"

Anson wasn't satisfied. "The Police, Sheriff, Texas Rangers, FBI, and Homeland Security, to name a few," he countered.

"If we find they plan violence, then we call in those folks. We're kinda' like Paul Revere."

"Let's get back to our plans," Charley injected. "We don't want to get caught up here using this room since we didn't ask for it. How about where our suspects spend the night, Phil?"

"Only a few reservations have been made so far. We're guessing who the bad guys...err, the suspects... are. The few reservations already made are at the same place, Mountain Inn."

"Well, keep after it, Phil. The Police, or whoever, will need names and home addresses of each one.

"Is your photo-taking on track, Roscoe? That's really important."

"Well, I had a setback. I took a slat out of the closet door I'll be behind, taking pictures. Replaced it with a strip of screen. Clarice caught me and made me put it back. Other than that, I'm ready and equipped to snap hundreds of photos."

Joe Cotton stood up. "Before you ask about my plan, I'm still looking for a kitchen to provide us a big pot of laxative-laced hot coffee. I may have to make it at home myself and cart it in. Anybody here have a big old GI mermite container that I can borrow? You know, the kind we used for taking hot chow to the field?"

"Why not make the coffee in the library's kitchen?"

"Too easy to track where it came from. We don't want the Library blamed if things go wrong. Jesse, how about you helping Joe with his coffee project?"

After a nod from Jesse, Charley asked the others for questions.

Phil's hand was up. "Another idea, once our suspects are tucked in the night before, how about a fire alarm to rouse them outta' their warm beds?"

Charley frowned. "You mean to actually start a fire at the inn?"

"No, of course not! Just trigger a fire alarm so they all have to evacuate during the wee hours."

Joe shook his head. "That would activate the Fire Department."

Someone else spoke up. "Everyone in the inn would have to get out, not just our suspects. Somebody might get hurt in the excitement."

"Thanks, but no thanks, Phil. Let's stick to what we got. Just get the names and addresses of them suspects."

TWENTY FIVE

Dan spotted Donitz sitting at a table in the back of the restaurant as he entered ten minutes late. Donitz strummed his fingers on the table, either uncomfortable with the surroundings or Dan's late arrival. They exchanged 'Good mornings.'

Donitz touched a formal black tie while regarding Roberts. "Thank you for your assistance with Madame, the Library Director, Mr. Roberts. Was she receptive to our complaints?"

Dan easily remembered Lara's angry reaction to his relaying the complaints, instead of Donitz. So he just nodded. "Said she would take care of them, Mr. Donitz.

"But it would be preferable, she said, were you to complain directly to her, rather than through me.

"Ahh...You mentioned another matter on the telephone?"

"Just so, Mr. Roberts. To our meeting this week we have invited a number of people residing in the Hill Country, as you call it. I hope to enlist them in our order, thus increasing our numbers and capabilities."

Dan waved at a waitress for coffee. "What are the capabilities of your study group, Mr. Donitz?"

"A shrewd question, Mr. Roberts. I admire your directness. That's one reason I think you might be interested in working with our group in safeguarding these possible new entrants to our order."

"How do you mean, 'safeguarding?'"

"I mean employing you to assist our most capable but overworked security officer, Mr. Bruno, in vetting these new initiates."

"If you are expecting an immediate reply, Mr. Donitz, I'd need to know more about the aims of your order."

Donitz nodded stiffly. "I brought a copy of our order's history which I think you will find interesting. Most Americans are fascinated by the history of the 'old country' as you call it.

"I suggest we meet again after you read this. Here also is a copy of the oath all initiates take upon entering our order."

A phrase of the oath held Dan's attention. "What does this mean, 'to initiate retribution upon those opposing our King and Kaiser, Frederick 1?"

Donitz touched his tie again. "It means there are always persons inimical to our ideals…"

"But 'retribution?'" Dan persisted.

"In any society, sir," Donitz fingers began drumming the table again, "there are malcontents standing in the way of progress. They must be assuaged…or eliminated. Your own 'War Between the States' is an example of that."

Donitz's expression changed as he rose from the table. "Would it be convenient for us to meet this evening and answer any further questions you might have? We will also consider an informal, although lucrative, contract for your assistance of Mr. Bruno. Here's my local number, please call and we'll have dinner at a place of your choosing."

Twenty minutes later, Dan stood outside Lara's door in the Library. He held a small crystal vase containing a single red rose.

He knocked and entered on hearing her "Good morning."

Recognizing his voice, she looked up from signing requisitions and receipts. "Hi, Dan. Have a seat. What's up?"

Carefully he placed the vase and rose on the corner of her desk and sat down. She noticed his grave expression. "Something wrong?"

He expelled his breath "I just had a meeting with that Mr. Donitz, at his invitation. He offered me a job, something to do with security of new initiates to his order who will be meeting in your Conference Room tomorrow."

She frowned. "I don't understand. He wants to employ you? I thought you said there was no connection between you two."

"There's not, but he says he has a job for me.

Contrary to what you think, I am not his lackey. I must tell you what he revealed about his 'order,' as he calls it. In answer to my questions, he gave me these two papers." He stood and laid them on her desk.

Not taking her eyes off him, she asked. "What's in them that's causing you to act so strangely, even bringing me a peace offering?"

He studied her. "That rose symbolizes my feeling for you, Lara. What these papers reveal is that Donitz and company are not just studying medieval history. They select people who may be enemies of their long-dead 'King and Kaiser' for *retribution!*"

"What?"

"His very word, Lara! They intend to eliminate those people who are somehow identified as 'inimical to their order.' That's exactly how he explained it to me just a few minutes ago!

"These people are coming to your Library tomorrow! We've got to do something!"

Tapping a pencil on the desk, Lara stared at him. "What do you suggest we do, Dan?"

He blurted, "We've got to inform the police...or someone."

"Have you evidence that someone has been killed, even threatened?"

"No," he admitted.

She stood behind her desk. "You remind me of someone else, right here in the Library. Like you, Charley's certain that the Donitz group worships devils or something worse.

ROY SULLIVAN

I've warned him and his buddies about interfering with Donitz's peaceful use of the Conference Room. I'm giving you the same warning!

"You really confuse me, Dan. First this man apparently befriends you and offers you work. Next you are calling him a terrorist...or something. That's duplicity!"

Wordless for once, he turned to leave.

"And take that damned rose and these papers with you!" she yelled.

TWENTY SIX

He found Charley loitering on a street corner near the Court House. "Buy you a beer?

"Yeah, man! That sounds great!" Charley's high spirits slightly lifted Dan's depression after the stand-off with Lara.

Minutes later they sat side by side at the Green Lounge on Water Street "What's the occasion?" Charlie mumbled, helping himself to a bowl of pretzels.

"Our Library Director just told me that you and I are kindred spirits, Charley. So here we are, conspiring. I want to tell you what I just found out about that Donitz bunch coming to the Library tomorrow."

Charley studied his beer. "This has to be confidential between you and me, understand? I'm in enough trouble with that lady already."

"Me, too. Charley. What can we do to force Donitz and his bunch to stay away...leave the Library alone?"

Charley loudly swallowed and set his beer bottle on the bar. "Are you serious? I gotta know before I tell you anything."

"I'm serious, Charley. I had a meeting with Donitz

an hour ago. He wants to hire me to help that security guy, Bruno. I asked, what was the purpose of his order?"

Dan looked around the deserted bar. "He told me they identify descendants of people who were enemies of an old German king named Frederick and..." he paused, "eliminate them!"

"Eliminate? You mean...?"

"That's right! He said there are 'malcontents, as he calls them, in every society and they *must be eliminated.*"

"Well, just as I figured! I knew there was something wrong with that bunch!" Charley leaned forward. "But we have plans to take care of them.

"First, you've got to swear to keep what I tell you under your hat."

For the first time that day, Dan grinned. "You're my role model, Charley. I'll not only promise that, I'll be there to help you!"

"Well," Charley snickered. "The only model I represent is male pattern baldness. Join us tomorrow morning at the Library and you'll see our plans unfold."

Although she wanted to go home and soak in a hot tub, Lara agreed to accompany Doris and Amy to happy hour at the Margarita restaurant. "I can't stay long," she insisted.

"A margarita or two will lift your blues," Amy promised.

"We'll celebrate that pay raise you got us!" Doris chortled, noting Lara's look.

"What's troubling you, Boss?"

They selected a table far from the entrance. "Here we'll have privacy to talk like real people." Doris tittered. "Not actors."

After ordering drinks and chips, Amy turned to Lara. "Are Charley and his clan worrying you?"

"No, I'm fine. Sorry if I seem concerned. I'm depending on Charley *not* to bother the Donitz group in the Library tomorrow. You're right. That pay raise next year is really something to cheer about!"

"Hooray!" Doris responded. "I'm ordering another round."

"No, you don't! My treat," Lara insisted, draining her glass. "Who wants to go home to a cold, lonely apartment?"

"Not us real people," Doris agreed. "I propose a toast to all the eligible young cowboys lurking somewhere out there! I know they're there, but *where*?"

It was past midnight when Lara unlocked her front door and sat heavily on the sofa She repeated Doris's question. "Where have all the eligible young cowboys gone?"

"One in particular," she lamented.

She turned on the CD and its first song deepened her mood:

"I want you to take me,
Where I belong...'
Where hearts have been broken..."

TWENTY SEVEN

Prompt as always, Bruno awakened his leader at 6:00 a.m. with coffee and a roll. An hour later, he walked the inn corridor where the membership candidates were housed, making certain they were up and on their way to the dining room.

"A busy day,' he mused, envious of Donitz's concern, which he thought excessive, for the twelve 'initiates.'

By 9:30 he had assembled the twelve in the van hired to transport them to and from the Library. This accomplished, he phoned Donitz that they were ready to depart from the front of the inn.

"Anything to report?" Donitz asked as he stepped aboard the van.

"Nothing of importance, sir."

"Explain."

"The clerk has misplaced our registration forms. I complained to the manager who assured me that the forms would be found and secured properly."

"Make certain it is done."

"Yes, sir!"

Donitz stood in the narrow aisle of the van and

reiterated what he told the twelve at dinner the previous evening. "This morning we will arrive at our destination in approximately twelve minutes. I will lead you through the Library front door, up a short stairway to the third floor where our meeting room is located.

"Neither stop nor speak to any person on the way to our room. In the past, some library patrons have evinced an unusual interest in who we are and what we are doing. Do not respond to such inquiries."

Once the twelve eventually were seated in the Conference Room, Donitz leaned forward to whisper the question Bruno always anticipated. "Is the room secured from clandestine listening and recording devices?"

"Yes, sir. However, I must report that during my earlier inspection I found a microphone hidden in the back of that device." He nodded toward the big wall-mounted TV.

"I removed it and the room is now secure."

"Excellent. Were you able to trace the microphone wire?"

"Only as far as a wall socket. I could not trace it farther without breaking into the wall.

Donitz frowned. "But we are secure?"

"We are, sir."

Donitz moved to a small podium to start the program. "I now ask you to rise and repeat with me the oath of loyalty to our revered King and Kaiser, Frederick 1."

The initiates, Donitz and Bruno stood and repeated the oath in unison.

'The same oath I gave to that Dan Roberts, whom I have not heard from since,' Donitz gritted his teeth.

Replacing his anger at Roberts with a stern look at the initiates, Donitz began a recitation of Frederick 1's antecedents and history of his reign in medieval Germany.

Pacing in front of the long table at which the twelve sat, Donitz raised his fist.

"Lest we forget, there remain to this day descendents of our liege's enemies. We continue to identify them for necessary retribution."

At these words, Bruno smiled for the first time.

Downstairs, Charley ranted at Amos. "No sound from that room? What about that fancy microphone you put in the back of the big TV?"

Amos splayed his hands. "Someone must have cut the wire. Sorry, Charley! I can't walk into the Conference Room now and fix it with all them sitting there!"

"No sound!" Charley clenched his fists and stared heavenward.

"No sound, no sweat, Charley," Joe Cotton quickly consoled. "When our free coffee arrives and they down a cup or two containing that laxative, they'll be goners," he chuckled.

"Gone to the toilets, then out the Library door!"
Joe raised his fists like a boxer.

"Who's at the door?"

Bruno opened it to investigate. After a few words in
the hallway, he returned, closing the door behind him.

"It's two men delivering us coffee."

Donitz bristled at the interruption to his lecture.
"Bruno, did you order coffee without telling me?"

"No, sir!"

"Who did?"

"The men outside are unable to tell me. They don't
wear restaurant uniforms, either. Perhaps the Library
ordered it for us?"

"We're taking no chances! It might be poisoned,
man!" He glared at Bruno. "Tell them to take the
coffee away. We didn't order it and don't want it!"

Bruno blanched. "But it's fresh, hot coffee…and
free!"

"Tell them to take it away! Far away!"

Joe Cotton stood in front of Charley, his face a
mixture of surprise and defeat. "You won't believe this
in a million years!"

In his kitchen chair, Charley suppressed a moan.
"What now? What won't I believe?"

"Those folks in the Conference Room turned
down our coffee! They refused to even let us bring
the mermite container into the room!"

Charley studied the ceiling again. "Then they must

have known it was doctored with laxative. How'd they know that, Joe? Who squealed?"

"I don't know," Joe almost wailed. "I'm sorry! How could they possibly know?"

"Maybe they're just extra cautious in there," suggested Dan, sitting across from Charley at the kitchen table.

"Don't look at me! I sure didn't tell them any of our plans."

"Our microphone, now the coffee plan, have failed." Upset, Charley rubbed his nose. "All we have left are their names and addresses from the inn and Roscoe's photos."

"How are we getting their photos?" Dan asked.

"Roscoe will take them from behind a closet door as they leave the Conference Room. We gotta' have those photos!"

"I'll go check with him to see if he's ready or needs anything," a determined Dan volunteered and departed for upstairs

Wearing the new red sweater dress intended to be worn to meet Mrs. Roberts, Lara sat beside Doris in the staff coffee room. "I see those German history buffs arrived and went quietly upstairs to the Conference Room. No adverse activity from Charley and company?"

Doris poured them both a fresh cup. "The day's not over, Boss. I'm keeping my fingers crossed. Meanwhile, the Brown Bag Book Club is in session downstairs and the Beginners' Water Color Class is splashing colorful Christmas cards all over the Young Adult room."

"Let's hope the Germans are out of our hair," Lara twisted a lock of her own, "on time."

Doris hesitated before changing the subject. "By the way, I saw your Mr. Roberts…"

Lara rolled her eyes. "He's *not* my Mr. Anything!"

"Okay, okay," Doris repressed a smile. "But I saw Mr. Nothing sitting in the kitchen talking to Charley a few minutes ago."

Donitz was pleased with the twelve initiates. So far they had been most attentive to his lecture about the order and Frederick 1. Even their questions had been predictable, even mundane, thus easy.

"If there are no more general questions, we will next examine the charter I have prepared for each of you to sign, attesting to your loyalty and service to our liege and leader, Frederick 1."

On a portable viewgraph screen, Bruno displayed the wording of the charter, leaving it in place for everyone to read. "As you see," Donitz pointed to several paragraphs after a few minutes, "you are acknowledging that you and your immediate family are lineal descendents of Frederick 1, thus owe him allegiance, loyalty, service and devotion.

"If you cannot freely and unequivocally adhere to these terms, you will be removed from our order at considerable risk to you. As I emphasized before, one of our objectives is the identification of descendents of the enemies of King Frederick 1 for possible punitive action."

To his surprise, there still were no raised hands, furrowed brows or angry faces among his audience.

At a nod from Donitz, Bruno carefully unrolled a large parchment replicating the viewgraph. At the bottom of the document was the printed name of each initiate.

"As Bruno calls your name, please come forward and sign the charter in the appropriate place." As Bruno began reading the names, individuals arose, came forward and solemnly signed their names.

"This concludes this initial meeting. I welcome you into the brotherhood of our august and noble order. Please quietly follow Bruno down the stairs to the van waiting outside. If there are people outside waiting to question or detain us, ignore them. We go directly from here to a festive banquet at our hotel.

"Again, I congratulate each of you on your selection and membership in our order. I assure you we will shortly raise our glasses to toast this momentous occasion.

"Now, please follow Bruno out the door and down the stairs to the van."

Bruno began leading the group down the hall, past a hallway closet and down the stairs. Once the room was empty, Donitz moved to the hallway. There, a slight noise caught his attention as he closed the Conference Room door behind him. He saw the elevator door down the hall closing with someone inside.

He rushed to the top of the stairs, excitedly calling to Bruno below and pointing downward. "Camera!"

Ousted from the kitchen by Clarice, Charley sat at a reference table with his partners brooding over their lack of success in ridding the Library of the "suspects."

Phil was the first to report. "I copied all their registration forms on my copier at the office and returned the forms to the inn's clerk. We can give the police the forms when we present the rest of our evidence against the suspects." He and Dan high-fived his success.

Amos shook his head, embarrassed about his report about the microphone in the Conference Room TV. Now there was no record of what was said inside the room to indicate the intentions--perhaps criminal--of the suspects.

Joe Cotton didn't want to volunteer his failure with the laxative-laced coffee, either. "They turned down our free coffee," he chewed his lip. "Making and transporting all that coffee to the Library was a bust."

"Ever determine why they refused the free coffee?" Anson asked.

"No idea, but nobody on my team gave it away." Joe eyed the others suspiciously.

"What did you do with all that tainted coffee?"

"We dumped it in the river behind the Library."

Counting the faces around the table, Charley

smacked his forehead. "Where's Roscoe? Anybody seen Roscoe? Where are his photos of the suspects?"

Dan Roberts lifted a hand. "I saw him maybe thirty minutes ago in his closet next to the Conference Room. Said he was rarin' to take their photos and didn't need anything. Maybe he's still in that closet?"

"Dan, go check on him, will ya'? Come back and let us know. Those photos are critical! Without them, all we have is a stack of registration forms to show for all our work!"

Dan Roberts went back to the third floor, to check if Roscoe was still in the hall closet, maybe adjusting his camera.

No Roscoe.

Downstairs, Dan checked the main floor, then the kitchen, to no avail. Outside, he walked around the playground where a group of youngsters were playing. He was about to return to the Library when a he heard,

HELP! HELP!

He saw a small boy in coveralls screaming at the far end of the playground near the river. He rushed to the sobbing child, who without a word, pointed to an overgrown sage bush.

A still figure sprawled behind the bush. Roscoe Waller lay there, eyes closed in a grimace, his chest covered with blood.

TWENTY EIGHT

He knelt and checked the still form. Roscoe was not breathing nor was there a discernible pulse. Dan shook his head, in disbelief. He had seen lots of dead bodies in Iraq but this was Carrville, Texas, USA! And near the Library! Lara's Library!

He dialed 911 with his cellphone to report finding the body and began answering the dispatcher's rapid questions.

"Yes, I said a dead body.

Behind the Library, right next to the river.

No, he is unresponsive and covered with blood.

Looks like a deep wound in the throat.

Dan Roberts. D-A-N-R-O-B-E-R-T-S.

I'm from Comfort, not Carrville.

Yes, I'll stand by until the police get here."

While he waited for the police, he backed off, seeing several footprints in the soft earth and grass. The area about Roscoe's body looked disturbed as if a struggle had occurred there. Dan tore pages out of his notebook to carefully mark each footprint to prevent its obliteration.

Looking about, he saw one of Roscoe's arms was flung forward, away from the torso. It appeared to point toward the river bluff, only a few feet away. Walking that way, he looked over a steep cliff and into the deep Guadalupe River.

Slamming his forehead, he remembered he should notify Lara to keep everyone out of the playground area.

"Lara, this is Dan. This is an emergency. Please don't hang up on me. I'm behind the Library, between the playground and the river, where I found a body.

"Yes, a human body. Please try to keep everyone away from here until the police arrive and take control.

"Yes, I've called the police and I hear a siren in the distance. Yes, Lara, I'm fine.

If you'll allow me, I'll come see you as soon as the police finish with me.

"No! I had nothing to do with this death! Who? Don't tell anyone, but it's Roscoe. The police will want to notify his next of kin themselves. Got to go now since the police just arrived."

To two policemen, Dan repeated his words previously given the 911 operator. A sergeant opened the patrol car door and motioned. "Get in. You've to go to the station to make a statement."

Dan looked at the officer. "Sure, but first you should extend that yellow crime scene tape all the way down around the cliff to the river. I think Roscoe threw his camera into the river, rather than give it up, before his throat was cut. And I need to go inside to tell the Library Director what's happened here and to keep people out of this area."

"Get in," the sergeant repeated. "We'll keep the library folks away. Our Chief's waiting to see you."

"What about the yellow tape?"

"Get in or I'll have to cuff you! You've been watching too much *Chicago PD*."

At police headquarters he was interviewed by two more officers who instructed him to begin a written statement. Finishing, he handed the pages to the two. "I have a theory," he offered.

"Thought so," one of the interrogators grinned. "Everyone does. What's yours?"

"As I said, I know the victim, Roscoe Waller. With his camera, Roscoe secretly was taking photos of the members of a suspicious group meeting in the Conference Room of the Library today.

"One of them must have seen him taking pictures and chased him out the back."

Smiling to themselves, one of the investigators asked, "Why would this mysterious person have done that?"

"He wanted to get the film from Roscoe's camera so there's no record of who was at that meeting. The man caught up with Roscoe near the river--you can see scuffle marks there--and stabbed him when Roscoe wouldn't surrender his camera.

"Maybe Roscoe threw his camera over the cliff into the river, instead of letting the assailant have it. You need to get a diver into the water under that cliff to search for the camera. Maybe even the murder weapon is there, too!"

"Maybe, maybe, maybe," one of the interrogators mimicked. "You're a person of interest…if not a murder suspect yourself…and we're keeping you here until we are sure what happened."

"May I use your phone?"

"Calling your attorney?"

"No, to call the Library Director. I promised her I'd call!"

Angry, Charley sat opposite Doris and Lara in the latter's office where he admitted the 'snorers' plans to "expose those suspects." The hired van, filled with the Donitz group, quickly disappeared down Water Street at the appearance of the police.

"I tell you," he sputtered, "there's something wrong with that bunch. What better proof do you want? Where's Roscoe? They may have hurt poor Roscoe because of them photos!"

Lara stopped his monologue. "How do you know anyone was injured? The police haven't told us anything."

Charley formed a temple with his fingers. "Roscoe's missing and Dan hasn't returned to tell us where Roscoe is. Maybe the police are questioning him right now."

"They'll be looking for you, too, Charley, if what you tell us is the truth. Why did you disregard our Library rules and warnings about bothering other patrons?"

"Those suspects aren't patrons! They're terrorists… or something. That's what we were trying to find out and tell the police!"

Amy opened the door without knocking. "The police are here and want to see you right away, Charley."

Still at the police station, Dan was being questioned by a new team of investigators including a just-arrived Texas Ranger. "Let's go over your statement again," one began.

"Explain why you were in the Library with this man…" the officer double-checked the name, "Charley Moss."

Dan drew a deep breath as he began repeating the now familiar words. "Charley suspected the strange group meeting today in the Conference Room was planning some kind of trouble. I was helping Charley and his buddies ascertain the intent…the plans…of the group. They claim to be studying medieval Germany, which we all think sounded suspicious."

"You think someone within that group was responsible for this…homicide?"

"Sure, I do. Roscoe's photos would identify the members meeting at the Library for possible use by you guys. If the group is subversive, it would do anything to prevent disclosure of those photos. To include murder," he added distinctly.

Another agent spoke up. "Did you witness anyone being followed or attacked?"

"No, sir. I said that earlier."

The agent looked up from a notepad. "If you did not see any attack, why did you say we should search the river for a camera?"

"I think destroying Roscoe's photos was their objective. Rather than give up the camera, I think Roscoe heaved it into the river. One of his arms pointed in that direction."

The Ranger, whose name tag read Gallegos, asked a question. "If that camera was so important to the killer, why didn't he or she retrieve it from the river?"

"He didn't have time. If it was in the river, he thought it never would be found and he was safe."

"Any further questions?" Gallegos asked, surveying the others.

"Apparently no more at this time, Mr. Roberts. You are excused but don't leave Carrville or your home without informing the Chief of Police's office. We may call on you for further questioning. Clear?"

An investigator raised a hand. "What about the press, Ranger?"

"Thanks, Fred. Since our investigation is incomplete, Mr. Roberts, please do not answer any press questions or make any statement concerning this homicide to anyone. Are we clear on that?"

"Yes, sir."

Dan immediately walked back to the Library to see Lara. Her greeting was his best yet.

"Certain you're all right?" She hugged him, looked into his eyes, then hugged him harder.

"I'm fine now," he whispered in her ear. "So good, I'm applying for a library job, to stay this close to you!"

TWENTY NINE

The next morning, Charley found Lara and Dan having breakfast together at the Norteno. Dan gestured and Charley joined them, spreading out the morning newspaper.

"Bet you haven't seen this." Charley pointed to the headline.

"MAN FOUND DEAD NEAR LIBRARY"

"The lifeless body of a local resident was found yesterday between Water Street and the Guadalupe River. Police have yet to identify the man, pending next-of-kin notification.

Although not declared a homicide, police cordoned-off the area where the body was found and ordered a diver to explore the nearby river.

An investigation is being conducted by the police and Texas Rangers. Authorities announced a briefing will be conducted at Police headquarters at 3:00 p.m., Wednesday."

Charley thrust thumbs into his suspenders. "The

boys and I were questioned several hours yesterday," he grinned. "They were tickled to get Phil's list of the suspects at the hotel. We gave them such good information that we're all going to that briefing... maybe even sittin' on the front row!"

Amid the popping of flash bulbs and glare of TV lighting, the Police Chief began the briefing the next day.

"The deceased was Mr. Roscoe Waller of Carrville," he announced. "Next-of-kin have been notified. The body was discovered Tuesday afternoon next to the Guadalupe River, just south of the library playground."

Lara and Dan sat together, holding hands. At the Chief's mention of her library, Lara, shut her eyes. "Why did he have to mention us?"

The Chief continued reading his notes, "We are investigating Mr. Waller's death as a homicide, following the coroner's autopsy report. Our investigation continues in coordination with the Texas Rangers and the Department of Homeland Security. Two persons of interest have been identified and are being sought for questioning. We do not know any motive at this time.

"Although our investigation is in early stages, I'll attempt to answer a few questions."

A female reporter was the first to respond. "Can you comment on the study group meeting at the

Library that day and any connection of it with Mr. Waller's murder?"

"No comment at this time," the Chief replied, glancing at his watch.

"Were there any signs of robbery?"

"No comment at this time. Our investigation is ongoing."

"Chief," another reporter signaled. "Can you tell us why there was a police diver in the river near the murder site?"

The Chief smiled. "We are making maximum effort to find any evidence to help solve this terrible crime as quickly as possible."

A tall man stood up, hand in the air. "Did your diver find any evidence?"

The Police Chief studied the man for a moment. "Yes, I believe so."

The same man's sudden follow-up question seemed to surprise the Chief. "Did you find that camera?"

"Ahh, yes, we discovered some very useful evidence."

"Are the photos intact?"

The Chief paused, without answering, and ended the briefing with the following.

"Further information will be available in a public information release tomorrow. I should add that we are grateful to a number of library patrons providing us with valuable background information on this case. Thank you," he nodded at Charley and others sitting on the front row.

That evening Dan and Lara stepped into the Margarita restaurant for drinks and dinner. She noticed a bulge in his shirt pocket, which she unsnapped.

She removed a small velvet box and held it up.

"Is this for me?"

He tried to grab the box but she was too fast. Turning in his grasp, she extracted a ring, extended her finger and slid on the ring.

All he could do--as she admired an outstretched, diamond-ringed finger--was to kiss the pulse point on her neck.

"Calf rope!" he admitted defeat.

She turned and kissed him repeatedly. "Let's eat in a hurry, love," she whispered. "We don't want to keep your mother waiting!"

THIRTY

Uneasy, Charley and Dan sat at a large table at Police headquarters. "Do you think they aim to arrest us for something?" Charley whispered.

Dan shook his head. "No idea why we were summoned here, Charley. Unless they think we're 'co-conspirators,' as Lara called us."

"Coffee, gentlemen?" The Police Chief entered followed by Texas Ranger Gallegos. Since both were smiling, so then did Charley and Dan.

"Black would be fine," they both answered. "Thank you."

A tray of cups and a pot were placed on the table and the men helped themselves.

"You're wondering," the Chief began after all their cups were filled, "why you are here."

Charley couldn't resist a retort. "We're just happy that we ain't in a cell."

"Well, you're here," the Chief smiled, "because Ranger Gallegos and I want to thank both of you privately for your assistance in solving our murder case."

"Solved?" Dan repeated.

"You'll see in our 3:00 p.m. release that we have arrested and are charging two individuals for the murder of Mr. Roscoe Waller.

"What you won't see in the release is what I'm about to reveal to you, privately.

'Privately' means you may not divulge this to the press or anyone else until the suspects are convicted. Is that clear to both of you?"

Charley and Dan both nodded, followed by "Yes, sir."

"Okay, then. We thank you, Mr. Roberts, for tipping us about where we might find Mr. Waller's camera. Just as you said, it was in the river with its photos intact. The last photo shows a man with a knife about to stab the victim. This individual, named Bruno, has been arrested and is in our custody. The District Attorney's office is preparing to charge Bruno with first degree murder today.

"A second individual, named Heinz Donitz, also arrested, will be charged as an accessory to murder.

"In absentia, we thank Mr. Waller for his photos of the individuals attending that meeting in the Library. Those photos have been passed to Homeland Security for investigation.

"Mr. Moss, we thank you, not only for your part with the photographs, but also for the names and addresses of the individuals attending that suspicious meeting."

Gallegos was first to stand and extend his hand. "Thank you for joining us for coffee, gentlemen. Please remember the Chief's warning about revealing to anyone what we told you here."

Gallegos winked at Charley. "Or you might get to inspect the interior of that cell after all!"

On the sidewalk, Dan and Charley climbed into Dan's pickup to return to the Library. "I didn't see any cell in there but I sure intend to keep out of 'em! Thanks for the ride, Dan. See you at the Library!"

On December 13, Ceci Garcia began excitedly jumping up and down in the break room. All the staff, except Lara, watched, puzzled by her happy antics.

"What's wrong, Ceci?" Eugenia worried. "Are you all right?"

"I won! I won! I won the pool on Lara's engagement date!"

Ceci waved the social page from the day's newspaper at them.

They listened as she excitedly read them an article from the paper:

Colonel and Mrs. B.F. Beyer, of San Antonio, announce the engagement of their daughter, Lara Diana, to Mr. Dan Roberts of Comfort, Texas. A June wedding is planned for the couple, following a honeymoon at an undisclosed location.

"Hooray! Doris clapped. "An excuse for another party!"

Printed in the United States
By Bookmasters